Praise for

SLEEPAWAY

"A compelling, propulsive apocalyptic novel that plunges into the heartland of human complexity. Written in careful, spare prose, with intelligence and wit, *Sleepaway* raises important questions about how we deal with sickness and healing and, most importantly, about the human condition. What a book *Sleepaway* is!"

—**BRANDON HOBSON**, author of *Where the Dead Sit Talking*

"Novels this haunting, this unsettling, are rarely delivered with the poetic grace on display in *Sleepaway*. Sweet lord—I was not ready. In the tradition of Saramago's *Blindness*, *Sleepaway* is as insightful as it is entertaining, and ultimately succeeds both as a post-pandemic metaphor and a page-turner. Renowned poet Kevin Prufer has created a novel that will grip the reader from its opening and continue to resonate long after its haunting last line is read."

—**MAT JOHNSON**, author of *Pym* and *Invisible Things*

"Prufer paints beautifully the solace of found family after loss, the ways we both fail and step up to take care of each other. In a poet's voice, here aches the bittersweet awareness of how few moments we have alive. Here glows how we choose to love in the moments we have left."

—**BRENDA PEYNADO**, author of *The Rock Eaters*

SLEEPAWAY

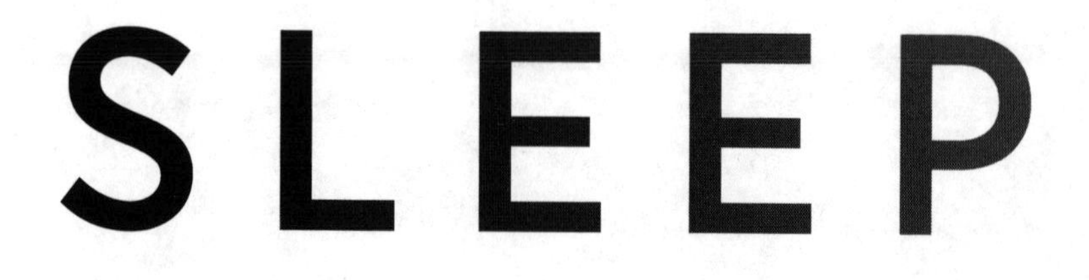
SLEEP

a novel

KEVIN PRUFER

ACRE
CINCINNATI 2024

Acre Books is made possible by the support of the Robert and Adele Schiff Foundation and the Department of English at the University of Cincinnati.

Printed in the United States of America

ISBN-13 (pbk) 978-1-946724-71-7
ISBN-13 (e-book) 978-1-946724-72-4

Designed by Barbara Neely Bourgoyne
Cover art: image from Unsplash

The press is based at the University of Cincinnati, Department of English and Comparative Literature, Arts and Sciences Hall, Room 248, PO Box 210069, Cincinnati, OH, 45221-0069.

Acre Books titles may be purchased at a discount for educational use.
For information please email business@acre-books.com.

For Diana

SLEEPAWAY

1 GLASS & SCOOBY

The invisible mists were falling, fine as pollen, and soon everyone would sleep.

+

Glass watched his temporary father clear the table of their lunch, then check his watch. He watched him close the refrigerator door with a kind of finality, knowing he might not open it again. He watched him gather the power tools from the deck and put them neatly away in the garage. He watched him take a quick drink of bourbon.

The mists had fallen a few miles south of town and now it was a matter of waiting. Glass sat on the back steps for a while with Carlos, who was fearless. Carlos was reading a comic book about giant ants with bright white teeth who lived in enormous anthills. Dangers lurked in their fluorescent passageways.

"Is that a wasp?" Carlos asked, pointing to a picture of what was, indeed, an anthropomorphized green-and-yellow wasp holding in one hand a laser gun and in the other an ant grub. "I'll have my dinner now," the wasp was saying.

"It's a wasp," Glass told him. "A mean-looking wasp."

Carlos had been interested in wasps since one stung him two weeks before. It was not a fearful interest, however. It was more of a cautious and abundant curiosity. Glass had watched him squatting over a pile of dirt on which several black wasps crawled tentatively, like blind men. He was learning about them, about their segmented, barbed legs, their prismatic eyes. And now here was a wasp among the good ants of *Antlandia*, which was the name of the comic book.

+

They could hear the alarm in the distance, an alarm that used to signal tornadoes, but had been repurposed now. Evening had already come on.

"It's OK, boys," Shane, Glass's temporary father, was saying from just inside the house. "Time to come in."

He smelled sweet, like bourbon. Little stars sparkled in the corners of Glass's vision already. Like a snowstorm, he thought, but when he turned his head to see the snow, the snow vanished. Then it was there again, at the edge of his field of vision, sifting over the old orange sofa in the living room, sifting over the neat stack of magazines on the coffee table.

His temporary father led the boys to the room they shared. He had made their beds and now they would climb in. Now the snow crowded Glass's vision and he tried to see through it, but he could not. With his hand he tried to wipe it away, but it would not be wiped away. His temporary father told him to take off his shoes and Glass lay on top of the blankets wearing his blue jeans and so did Carlos and his temporary father was saying, "It's OK. It's OK, boys," and then he lay down on the floor between the two beds and all three of them closed their eyes for almost exactly two minutes.

+

This is what Glass learned from people who said they knew about the mists: the mists had been designed in a Sinaloan lab by Russian scientists who were covertly creating a weapon that would destabilize but not permanently harm large populations. Or the mists were a kind of yellow pollen that floated on warm winds over the globe. The mists were spores that rose from wet and chemically damaged earth and got in one's nose and throat. The earth had cut right through a vast mist in space so the mists settled into the atmosphere as massive clouds of sleep. Every little spore was a sin and the mists were therefore all our sins' visitation upon us. The mists were justice and punishment and retribution and a kind of cleansing. All at once.

+

Glass had once been a normal boy who spent an abnormal amount of time sitting in the middle school hallway because he could not hold still. He just couldn't. Every inch of his body craved movement when he was at school. Rorkisha had asked Glass how to spell *spaghetti* and Glass had almost spelled the whole word when his teacher told him this was the last time, the final time, and now Glass would have to sit outside the classroom door on the cold floor until he could learn to be still and stay quiet.

So Glass sat in the hallway, but he soon grew bored and rose and peeked through the little window into the classroom. Rorkisha caught his eye and smiled knowingly. Then, certain the teacher had forgotten about him, he wandered the hallways, drinking from each water fountain, finding his way to the area where the older students' classrooms were, wandering into the little empty science classroom, light sparkling in from the window and glittering over the stainless-steel countertops.

In one cabinet Glass found the knives they used to dissect frogs. He rubbed his thumb over a blade, and then he was looking at the life-size plastic skeleton, and then at a strange thing floating in a jar, the lungs of a cat, the label said. A cat's lungs. This was fascinating, and he observed it from all angles. The lungs floated like a dead lamprey, like gray meat, and when he looked closely he could see the intricate mottled surfaces, pink and gray, as the lungs turned in the formaldehyde.

+

What can be done about Glass? What can be done? He just couldn't be still. His teachers sipped bad coffee in the teacher's lounge and shook their heads then moved on to better topics: the girls' soccer team's unusual run of success, the school's leaking roof, the theft of a TRS-80 computer from the Remedial Education Center.

When the other students read silently, Glass would mouth the words and then, without realizing it, speak them aloud. Once, when the teacher's attention was focused on something else, Glass got out of his seat and went to the window and looked down into the sunlit parking lot where someone had parked a classic car of some kind—big and black and square. "It's a Model A," he exclaimed to no one. He was a pleasant boy, no doubt about it, and not exactly dumb, though he'd been held back one grade and might be held back another. It was as though a purely physical joy had entered his body and could manifest itself only in distraction and speech. And he could get nothing done.

We don't quite know what to do about him, they'd told his father, Olaf, who didn't know what to do, either. And neither did Margaret, his father's girlfriend, who tried to take an interest. She really did. He was, after all, such a pleasant boy.

+

He hadn't meant to drop the jar on the floor—he'd been surprised by the older kids rushing into the classroom and it had just slipped from his hands. Now the lungs were fat gray slabs on the linoleum among glass shards. The smell of formaldehyde filled him.

So Glass had been sent home, and what was his father going to do with him? He had classes to teach, and mostly Glass remembered him shaking his head, saying, "Really? A goddamn cat's lungs?" and then packing the boy off with him to his office at the university, where he would twirl in his father's desk chair while his father lectured on Native American cultures and, really, it was in that moment that Glass was happiest, there in his father's office that smelled of old books and mold and human bones and copy machine toner.

That was a happy day in his life, when he had broken the jar on the floor. It was months ago now. His father was gone now.

There had been so many *things* that awful year—his father slipping irretrievably into sleep and nowhere for Glass to go, certainly not to his mother's little efficiency apartment in Minnesota, or wherever that useless woman was living now. And probably not to Margaret. And then Shane, his father's closest friend in that town, had volunteered. His temporary father.

+

Before he fell permanently asleep, Glass's father taught archaeology at the university. He had a little beard and mustache and he raised his eyebrows playfully when he spoke, as if everything he said had a door in it, a door to another room that Glass would never get to see.

Glass spent weekends with his father and the graduate students excavating Indian bones and artifacts from the plowed hills around town. All day they'd dig and sift and walk the long rows of corn looking for scrapers or cores or projectile points or even the littlest flakes of flint that glittered blackly in the sun and signaled that tool processing had taken place here many hundreds of years ago.

In the evening, at home, his father would wash the finds in the sink and bake them dry in the oven before bringing them to the lab in their basement, where he sorted them into little gray boxes or onto clear plastic trays, marking each with indelible fine-point black pen: find location, depth, weight, etc.

In the basement, vast, gray metal shelves lined the walls and on some shelves were gray boxes filled with flint artifacts and on other shelves were human bones—long boxes of femurs, tibias, finger bones. Rows of skulls.

One skull had a quarter-size hole right in the forehead. Glass remembered looking at that and imagining the tomahawk that inflicted it. The death blow, his father had told him. The death blow, the death blow, Glass repeated to himself. The hole was deep and black and the skull had perfect yellow teeth. He pushed his finger through the hole, right into the absence of brain.

+

Anyway, the skulls were in the dark basement and the house was locked up. Though Shane had taken Glass there a few times to get more of his things and Glass had wandered around familiar rooms, the house smelled different without his father in it. Gone was the lingering scent of tobacco mixed with laundry detergent, sardines, old red wine, Four Roses bourbon, and bug spray. Now it smelled of bleach and Pine-Sol—someone had sent in a cleaning crew—so he hurried through the neatened-up living room into his bedroom and gathered together a few more books, a photo album, his collection of ancient Roman coins, a handful of glitter pens, while Shane paced in the kitchen because soon they'd have to pick up his real son, Carlos, from his swimming lessons.

Sometimes Glass studied Shane's relationship with Carlos, which was complex and not all good. He gathered that Carlos lived with Shane during the school year and with his mother during vacations. Sometimes Shane doted on the boy. Other times he disappeared completely into his work or, in the evenings before the boys went to bed, he drank and grew vague. Grew vaguer still after the boys were asleep, Glass assumed, because he wasn't blind. He could see the empty bottles of scotch in the garbage can.

Carlos's mother was "getting settled" in Cleveland, where she had some job or other, and for now, Carlos would spend the school year here and summer with her, though that was all a little tentative and would depend on his mother's situation.

Almost every night Carlos's mother called long-distance. She'd exchange a few quick words with Shane. "Yeah," Shane would say into the phone. "Yeah. Yes. Of course. I've got a backup plan. Of course I do. And if he needs to come to you—yes, of course he will. I said he will, dammit." And then he'd hand the phone to Carlos, who would say, "Hi Mama, hi," and then he'd speak eagerly with her, quickly, in a low voice so Glass couldn't hear, winding the telephone cord around his little body as he spoke, then unwinding, winding and unwinding.

It was clear to Glass where Carlos would rather be.

+

The alarms always surprised Shane, scrolling up the television's blue atmosphere, fizzing through the radio's gray half-static: at this time, everyone was to return home. At this time, no one was to be on the road, in a car, operating dangerous equipment. A sleep was coming, another sleep was coming, they were falling asleep in Sedalia, they were falling asleep in Knob Noster, get to a safe place where you can lie down comfortably, where you will not drive into a tree or a school, a place where you can close your eyes for one or even two minutes, where you might not, like Glass's father, wake up at all.

And so Shane had checked the thermostat and put the two boys, who were already seeing familiar snow flurries in the corners of their eyes, to bed, and he had lain on the gym mat between them. As he had done before and as he would have to do again and again, he knew it.

Because the sleeping had first been reported on the western coast of Mexico, the newscasters in those days called it the Sinaloan condition or, occasionally, the Sinaloan sickness, though it was not clearly a sickness.

Two years earlier, several thousand people near Rosario, Sinaloa, had fallen suddenly asleep and stayed that way for about thirty seconds. Some of the cars on the 280 had merely slowed to a stop as the drivers relaxed into slumber, but more of them had wrecked, their drivers sleeping heavily through injury, some of them into death.

Had an airplane been flying above that part of Mexico at that moment, everyone on board would also have slumped forward, the plane propelling onward, pilotless for thirty seconds.

The Sinaloan condition had spread quietly, those toward the edges of affected areas slipping into mere seconds of sleep, those beyond the edges experiencing only fatigue, an overwhelming desire to rest their heads on their steering wheels even as they drove home from work.

No one knew precisely why the Sinaloan condition would suddenly afflict one area intensely, then always move with the direction of the wind, everyone in its path falling into brief sleep, everyone on its edges slipping into ennui, fatigue, depression. After a while, the wave would disappear and most everyone would wake up—though a few might remain asleep forever, unrousable.

This was very rare at first.

+

Were animals affected? Mostly not at all. Birds never rained from the sky, battering the hoods of cars, defacing parking lots, or crashing through skylights. Fish didn't sink in schools to the bottoms of lakes to suffocate in rich mud. Animal populations, it seemed, were resilient and largely immune.

With one exception: Certain breeds of pig—American Yorkshire, Breitovo, Saddleback—were known to grow strangely listless during the sleeping events and later, when things grew much worse, were remotely videotaped tumbling, hundreds at a time, to their sides in the mud and grass, lying immobile, eyes wide open, for several minutes before righting themselves and going about their business.

Of course, with no one awake to witness these events, much of the animal response to the Sinaloan condition remained conjectural, deduced but unobserved. It is, in fact, still somewhat conjectural to this day.

+

This was in 1984, before iPhones or Facebook or Twitter or UrNewz. Not many had conceived of the internet then. Not Shane nor Olaf. Only Glass could have conceived of it, and only because he read books in which an enormous computer, the Microvac Z100, had reached into every living room through the television sets and was quietly controlling the minds of every family on Earth. He had read through the first six books in *The Microvac Chronicle*s twice, following the story of a girl brave enough to turn away from the televisions, to set forth on a mission to find the secret location of Microvac itself, to learn why it had been created, to what diabolical purpose it was bent, and, ultimately, to turn it off. Along the way, she made many strange friends, discovered a secret Microvac-resistance group, learned of a device that fit almost invisibly into one's ear that counteracted the mind-control, risked her life among snowy mountains and, later, was pursued by strange government agents in brown suits. These were good books, and the seventh was still to be published.

Still, in Glass's mind, there was no internet, only the possibility of one. People lived much more separate lives back then, alone with their thoughts and conjectures, which they shared at coffeehouses by the train tracks or late at night on the telephone, twisting the phone's cord with their fingers. "They were falling asleep in Jones Bend last night." "Jones Bend, really?" "That's what I heard. And it lasted almost two minutes." "Two minutes?" "Almost." "Getting longer and longer, ain't they?"

+

That the Sinaloan condition seemed to affect those of European descent more strongly than those of other genetic lineages was, at first, a curiosity of the syndrome. In this way, it resembled Tay-Sachs or sickle cell: certain populations, for one reason or another, were far more susceptible to severe cases. Of course, everyone suffered from the sudden ennui or, nearer the epicenter of each event, total sleep. But those who could not wake up were statistically much more likely to be fair-skinned, to have ancestors from Germany or England or Ireland, or any of the European nations. And they were rarely, though occasionally, children.

Glass didn't think too much of this, though his friend Scooby brought it up now and then, by way of making fun of him.

"My part of town," Scooby said, "gonna go on just fine in these sleeps," and then he'd laugh, because he was right.

The town had two main parts, like many an American city in miniature: a section of well-maintained ranches and bungalows and the occasional Queen Anne, elaborate and expensive to heat. And then that part of town made up of unimpressive two-story apartment complexes, former motels, or once prosperous cottages gone to rot, unmaintained, old sofas on the front porches on which old men sat. Here were the transient day laborers, who lived for the harvest season in the half-abandoned Econo Lodge, before moving south and east in their pickup trucks and minivans to the next Econo Lodge in the next town. Here were not the trucking executives, but the men who maintained the trucks.

But there was only one junior high in town, and Scooby and Glass were often seen circling the playground during recess, talking, their eyes on the ground. Once, Scooby had found a five-dollar bill, and another time Glass had found a gold-plated cuff link with a single bright blue stone in the center of it. They talked about science fiction and TV and *The Microvac Chronicles* and, increasingly, the sleeping that descended upon them.

"We're gonna wake up, over where I live, but not you," Scooby once said, kicking an old bottle so it skittered across the concrete.

"I know it," Glass said.

They walked in silence for a few moments. Then Scooby turned to Glass and smiled and said, "I'm only kidding. We're all gonna be fine. All of us."

And Glass smiled back, because what did he know? What did anyone know?

+

What no one knew—what Glass had tried to explain—was that *his* Sinaloan condition was different from that of the other people he knew. In the beginning, he, like everyone else, experienced the diagnostic shooting stars at the periphery of his vision, the strange sparkling that eventually filled his vision. But unlike others, the sleep he fell into was not dreamless. And when the others woke from their first sleeps talking of the overwhelming blackness of their experience, their complete anesthetization, Glass tried to explain that he had had such vivid dreams, more vivid than anything he had experienced in normal sleep, though even in normal sleep he was a restless boy.

In Glass's Sinaloan dreams, he was no longer a twelve-year-old boy, but a little bit older. His father was there, too, his voice husky and deep, and he smelled of snuff and mint. And they were in a town that felt familiar in the dream, but strange upon waking, a desolate town, an overgrown little park near the town hall, the sky streaked with gray, a late-afternoon light, a feeling of May in the air. It threatened to rain but it would not, and Glass and Glass's father and perhaps a hundred others were settling into folding chairs spread out on the grass, because the show was about to begin.

I was there with them, sitting just a row behind Glass and his father, and when Glass glanced at me, I quickly looked down at my program.

+

Sometimes Shane would take Glass to visit his father in the sleep ward of the hospital. Every hospital had one then. And in some places, they were expanding, sleep wards edging onto other floors, other areas. And Glass would stand over his father's bed squeezing a can of ginger ale, not sure what to do with himself, what to say. Olaf simply slept, a little IV tube offering him nourishment. His face was paler, but still full. His beard had grown, little hairs sprouting around his ears.

"I don't know what to say," Glass told Shane, and Shane said, "You don't have to say anything at all."

But here was a situation in which one ought to say *something*, if only Glass knew what. And not knowing, Glass told his father part of the plot of *The Microvac Chronicles*, a scene in which Amanda, the heroine, realizes that something has been amiss in her neighborhood ever since the cable company installed those free silver boxes onto the backs of the television sets and screwed new gleaming antennae high on the telephone poles. Amanda had watched them, wondering what they were doing, what those silver boxes and antennae could be for.

Still Amanda came home from school each day and watched TV with her friends, not noticing at first how her friends were changing. Their behavior had become more rhythmic. They repeated the same phrases, the same slang terms, unfamiliar to her, over and over again. They were in sync with one another in a way Amanda could not understand. Yes, they retained some fraction of their personalities, but their concerns had evolved since the antennae were installed—a rebellious spirit had lifted. They wore makeup and dressed similarly—French cuffs and black wayfarer sunglasses and tortoiseshell barrettes and legwarmers. And Amanda, who had always been unconventional, with her collection of rare bottlecaps and antique medicine bottles, found herself increasingly isolated.

One day a powerful storm swept through Midvale, a storm that shook the houses and tore trees from the ground, a storm that knocked the power and cable lines, sparking and fizzing, into the street. When the power failed, Amanda was at a sleepover party, where her friends seemed suddenly to blink alertly, to come to themselves, stunned and strange, wiping pink lip gloss from their mouths as they peered at themselves awkwardly in the mirror. What am I doing here? they asked. Who are you? They looked at one another in awe, as if they had been asleep for many months and only now were waking up. Amanda, confused, tried to explain that they were at Janey's house, that it was a sleepover for her birthday. But her friends just stared, bewildered. Later, when the power was restored, when the lights suddenly blinked back on, their faces twitched a little, their eyes rolled back, and they returned to the empty selves they had been just before the storm.

That was how Amanda came to know they were being controlled. That was how she came to leave Midvale and eventually to join the Microvac underground resistance movement.

All this Glass told his father, who showed no sign of having heard anything at all. Sunlight filtered through the window into the vague hospital room.

"Time to go," said Shane, looking at his watch.

+

"I don't know that you need to take him to see Olaf even once a week," Shane's sister was saying. "I mean, if he doesn't even move, if he's completely asleep." She stood in the doorway, cleaning her glasses again with a piece of old paper towel.

Shane nodded at that, but he wasn't really listening. He was trying to watch the news. Last year, the average sleep time during a Sinaloan incident had been just over a minute. Now it was nearing three minutes, doubling every nine months. The newscaster looked grave, but then brightened, saying, "Now, in other news," moving on to a story about a local high school band and its mascot, a pygmy goat.

"I mean, if he's completely asleep," she was saying again, "really, what's the point?"

"The kid talks to his dad," Shane said. "He tells him stories from books he reads." He leaned his head back as far as it would go on the sofa, then closed his eyes, as if he'd had a very hard day, though, in truth, it hadn't been that hard. He'd taught a morning seminar at the university, lingered a bit drinking coffee in a cigarette-scented faculty lounge, had a couple glasses of something stronger on the way home at the VFW bar, where they let him drink though he was a veteran of no war.

His sister chewed on her pencil. She told him she had come by to do some laundry, that her machine was broken again, but he knew she was also curious.

"He's never going to wake up," she said. "None of them are."

"You don't know that," Shane said, head still tilted back on the sofa, eyes still closed. "They're working on a cure all the time."

That last part Glass overheard from the next room, where he'd just turned off the television. He knew she might be right. Her having said it didn't add to his troubles.

+

Olaf's sleep was almost completely black, though sometimes he could hear in the vast distance the rise and fall of voices. The words were never clear, like a voice heard through thicknesses of cotton. It was sometimes the voice of a boy and sometimes the voice of a woman.

+

Sometimes Glass would ride his bicycle five blocks to the house he used to live in with his father. He had a key. He would let his bike fall on its side on the grass and walk right in through the front door. Then he would sit in his quiet bedroom and page through his books, or walk into his father's room and stand at the foot of his bed looking at the deep blue bedspread, the heavy bedposts, the bedside table.

In the top drawer of the bedside table, he found lip balm, keys, receipts, a glue stick, several pairs of reading glasses, a bag of triple-A batteries, a canceled passport, a half-full silver flask, and a picture of himself from last year, one of those school photos.

He'd forgotten it was photo day and so had worn overalls and an orange T-shirt when all the other boys wore pastel button-downs and Izod shirts. He looked, his father said, like a farmer. And then he laughed, a kind laugh. It didn't matter. Glass fingered a set of keys he didn't recognize, then slipped them back in the drawer.

In the basement, the gray boxes of Indian artifacts loomed on their shelves. The rows of skulls, each cleaned and catalogued and marked in cramped black lettering, stared at him. He lingered on the one with the hole just above the left eye. The skull lingered on him, too, examining his pale little face, his wind-rumpled brown hair.

+

The alarms were going again, but this time Glass was at school, quietly drawing a variety of ducks in the margins of his textbook, *The Dog Next Door: A Reader*. The story they were reading had, in fact, been about ducks, about one particular duck who decides he is not *really* a duck, but a parrot. It was, in Glass's opinion, a stupid story. And then the distant sound of the siren, like a finger circling a wineglass's rim until it sang, high and shrill.

Mrs. Kogan said from the chalkboard, "OK, put your books away and your heads on your desks. Heads on your desks, heads on your desks," then walked briskly toward a cot in the corner of the room and settled back.

And just as she did that, the snow squalls began in the corners of Glass's vision, more and more snow until he lowered his head onto the desk and quietly returned to the strange park, the rows of gray metal folding chairs, the little makeshift stage, and his father beside him saying, "I guess they'll begin the play at any time," scratching at his ankle where a mosquito must have bitten him.

+

And just as dusk had almost settled and the sounds of night insects began to fill the air, a spotlight opened like an eye on the little stage in Glass's dream. A young woman was sitting on a tattered sofa in what looked to be a small apartment. Two suitcases sat by the front door, a large one and a smaller one, and the young woman paced nervously back and forth in the little living room.

"Hello?" she called. "Hello?" but the room was silent. So she opened the window and called down to the street, "Hey, you down there?" but again she got no response, so she closed the window and began to pace again.

Here I am, Glass wanted to say from the audience. *Here I am*. But he said nothing, because it was a play. He was at a play with his father. He was sitting in the dark with his father in front of the glowing stage and I was not even a thought to him, sitting in the row behind him, so close I could have touched his shoulder. But I didn't.

His father had taken him to a play and afterward they would drive home, talking about it. Lightning bugs hovered and glowed around them, yellow and white. Such crickets.

On the stage, a boy about Glass's age, but taller, bigger, this boy was coming through the apartment door.

"Where were you?" the young woman said. "We needed to leave twenty minutes ago! The minibus is packed. We've got to go!"

"I didn't hear you," he said, "or I woulda come sooner."

+

Then he was waking up again, lights sparkling at the edges of his vision, slowly clearing as he lifted his head. Already Mrs. Kogan had risen from her cot and the other kids were glancing around the room, rubbing glitter from their eyes—all but one girl who still hadn't moved.

Her name was Tonya. She had her head in her hands, her mussed brown hair swept to the side so Glass could see her flushed cheek and watch her breathe quietly. In her left hand she held a bright purple pen.

She still wouldn't move.

The other kids had noticed her, too, but they didn't get out of their desks. Certainly she should have been awake by now, and Mrs. Kogan strode across the room to her, touched her shoulder. "Tonya?" she said. "Tonya?" And when she did this, Glass remembered having addressed his father in those tones that day months ago, how his father hadn't moved, how he'd shaken him, how the sunlight filtered through the curtains over his face and Glass had tried to roll him on his back but he was so heavy and he wouldn't move and Glass's tone became more urgent.

And now the other kids were completely silent. Glass could hear voices from the classroom next door, could hear the hum of the clock on the wall while Mrs. Kogan gently shook Tonya then snapped her fingers by her little pink ear and the class drew its breath, waiting, watching.

Then Tonya moved a little bit, her grip tightening on the purple pen, and she coughed.

"Tonya?" Mrs. Kogan said once more.

"Yeah," Tonya said sleepily. "Yeah, I'm awake."

+

Most of the other kids liked Glass, though Glass was thin and small. But Glass had only one good friend. Scooby lived in a neat little house on the other side of town, the Black side, Glass's father called it. Scooby was called Scooby because it had been his father's nickname before him, but he didn't think about it too much. He was Scooby Franklin. It was the name his father called him.

Scooby's father, Miles Franklin, owned the Metropolitan Club, which was neither metropolitan nor a club. It was a windowless bar on the edge of town where workers went after they cleaned and parked the rigs in the vast black parking lots of Chickasaw Trucks. Scooby's mother taught second grade, or sometimes first grade. She had never been Glass's teacher, though.

Scooby was therefore left to his own devices most afternoons, and sometimes into the evenings. When they could, Glass and Scooby rode their three-speeds around the edges of town or over by the railroad tracks where they'd place pennies on the tracks for the trains to flatten. Sometimes they climbed down by the abandoned trestles where the boulders also were.

No one kept much track of the boys, Shane teaching evening classes, Scooby's parents at work. Sometimes Carlos tagged along and sometimes he didn't.

Below the trestles was a creek, and in the creek you could sometimes find flint artifacts, which Glass understood well and which interested Scooby enormously. They would take off their shoes and wade around the rocks and boulders, clearing away masses of rotting leaves and sometimes finding an archaic flint drill or curved scraper. Once, Glass had found a wet and rotting box of checkbooks someone had probably thrown from the bridge upstream. Another time, Scooby had split open a football-size hunk of shale to find inside it the perfect, delicate fossil of a millions-of-years-old fern.

On this particular day, though, they were finding nothing. It had been months since Glass's father had been awake and he'd been doing a little better in school, was passing four of his six classes and was getting high marks in language arts. It was a beautiful day, sun filtering through the leaves and mottling the earth.

Scooby, though, was tired and cranky. He had cracked open a half dozen rocks and found nothing inside them. He looked and looked for fossils in the shale and found nothing but gray pebbles and pop cans and a woman's soiled and wet brassiere hanging from the branch of a tree.

And then he saw something silvery bobbing in the current, caught among the rocks a dozen yards away. At first, he thought it was part of a car, maybe a chrome bumper, just a section of it rising out of the water, the rest caught among the rocks, but as he drew closer, he knew it was cans. Silver cans fastened together in plastic rings, cans of beer, a six-pack of National Bohemian beer.

Someone had set them in the water to keep them cool, hunters or high school kids, perhaps, and now here they were, caught and bobbing among the rocks. "Yo, Glass," Scooby shouted. "Lookit!"

Soon Scooby and Glass were giggling and tipsy, wading in the fading yellow light, swimming now where the creek became more like a river, so tipsy that they did not hear the alarms wailing in the far distance. They were on their third beer and peeing into the current and laughing and floating on their backs.

Then, one after the other, the two boys went limp in the water, fast asleep.

2 A WAITRESS NAMED CORA

Early on, Cora knew that, while the frequency of onsets of the Sinaloan condition was regular—about one event every twenty to thirty days in most locations—the average duration of sleep was increasing, with occasional large spikes. And all this increased the possibility that one might not, in the end, wake up at all. What began as a minuscule risk had become a little more serious as the tornado sirens rang at the edges of town and people pulled their cars over to the side of the road or lay back on the sofa or turned off the oven. Especially, though not exclusively, if your genes were like Cora's: German and English and a little Romanian.

What if I don't wake up? What if I never wake up? Dread consumed her when she remembered the white and gray stars glimmering in her vision, because unlike influenza, the Sinaloan condition didn't prefer the elderly or the infirm. It was, when it came to strength and firmity, impartial, taking from here a healthy young woman and from there a decrepit old codger, though passing over children, who would fall asleep with everyone and only extremely rarely fail to wake up.

Cora visited the overflow room only once, when a good friend, a former boyfriend, fell into sleep while rowing his little green dinghy one sunny spring day at Pertle Lake. By the time the dinghy had drifted to shore and a couple walking their dog found him, he'd been asleep for many hours, a bright pink sunburn on his pale face, which, when she finally saw him, had peeled badly.

The overflow room had once been the hospital's cafeteria but now was stripped of tables and counters and ovens. A smell of antiseptic and human sweat overwhelmed the scent of the cafeteria, the old roast beef. The sleepers lay still on their rows of cots, perhaps fifteen of them in all. Every now and then, one of them shifted, stretched, scratched herself. Bags of pale-yellow fluid—a kind of nourishment, she supposed—dangled from poles. The air was close until someone opened a window. Two nurses hung about, at times walking among the sleepers, seeing to the removal of stale bedding or waste. The sleepers slept on and on, not at all unhappily. Merely, it seemed to her, at peace.

But it was this peace that horrified her. When she looked down at her friend's pink face, the skin peeling from his nose—someone had rubbed it with lotion, a kindness—what she saw was a man she had known since she'd moved to town two years ago, fully embodied and alive. Not lost, but resting. Not a shell, but *him*—except unreachable, unable to be troubled by her. It was terrifying.

In those days, every little Missouri hospital had an overflow room. It was just something people knew about.

Everyone went on with the work of living, waiting tables and teaching classes and driving long-haul trucks between the cities or making deliveries between the towns. The company that made uniforms—the largest employer in that town—went on making uniforms for schoolchildren, sports teams, restaurants. The train came through, as always, though the town's active population slipped slightly as the overflow room grew just a little.

+

But I should get to the important part of the story: how Cora came upon those two boys floating on the river. One was faceup, the other facedown.

She had heard the sirens where she sat on a boulder on the riverbank, reading, so she knew that the invisible mists were already falling over the town. By then people had begun calling what came next simply a *sleep*, as in, "I hear another sleep is coming," or "I heard they had a sleep over in Columbia the other day."

Sometime later, she rose and walked a little way upriver, pocketing her book, knowing that by now everyone else was waking up, was just rubbing the sleep and glitter from their eyes and looking around the schoolyards or offices or grocery stores, was rising from the floor or turning the key again in the ignition or smiling, embarrassed, in the parking lot. She had a slight headache. She always did after the mists came down. And just beyond a gap in the trees, she happened to see what she thought were two bundles of laundry floating in the creek.

But it wasn't laundry. One of the bundles was suddenly moving, was grabbing at the other one and trying to flip it over. And when he finally managed it, Cora could see that these were two boys. And then she was wading out into the water, too, and helping the awake boy drag the unconscious boy to the shore.

The awake boy—he was white, slim, slight, had two scars on his face—was crying as she bent over the other boy—he was Black and a little heavyset and lay on the pebbles not breathing.

"Is he going to wake up?" the crying boy asked, but she couldn't answer him. It was as if the birds in the woods had become terribly loud, were filling her head, and she tried to remember what to do, because if the other boy were asleep, he'd be breathing. But he wasn't breathing.

She pressed down on his chest hard a couple times, but it felt futile and the slight boy was crying beside her and the birds kept getting louder while she pressed down on his chest again, harder, and blew into his mouth. She remembered that from Girl Scouts many years ago, pressing the flat of her palms into the plastic resuscitation dummy and blowing into its mouth, how everyone giggled at that and she'd felt a little stupid as she pounded on the plastic and rubber torso.

And then the faintest trickle of liquid slipped from the boy's mouth—his lips were growing pale—and he seemed to gasp. Or she imagined he gasped.

The sunlight yellow and dimming and she pressed again and then he really did gasp and more water came out of his mouth and then he was coughing and the other boy sat cross-legged on the stones, crying, looking at his friend.

It was then that she recognized the boys as the ones who sometimes rode their BMX bikes around the courthouse near where she worked. She'd once seen them in the parking lot with their plastic remote-control cars, racing them around and around and crashing them into the tires of parked cars. She'd liked seeing them. It made her happy that a white kid and a Black kid could be good friends; it gave her a kind of hope.

Anyway, I'm telling this story now because later on, when things get much worse, you will understand why Glass came to seek her out. Not because he knew her, but because he had decided to notice her, too. And, of course, she had saved Scooby's life.

+

In those days, Cora was a waitress at the Black Walnut Pub, hardly the worst job she'd ever had, though nothing like what she'd dreamed of, either. She was twenty-four and she wasn't from anywhere near town, but had drifted there from Nebraska. That's how she explained herself, anyway, gesturing vaguely: "I just came to town one day and thought I'd spend a little minute here, and then I *stayed*." Here she'd widen her eyes in a sort of mock horror, then laugh, because it really was inexplicable. How had she gotten here? She'd been here two years!

The truth was her aunt had been right all along, that a graduate degree in dramatic writing was, actually, quite worthless, at least when it came to making a living. And if you hadn't moved to town to work at the uniform company or Chickasaw trucking, then you came for the university, so she'd come, with her degree, for a job teaching four or five sections of English composition to the reluctant sons and daughters of farmers or small-business owners or airmen from the air force base. And after only one year of Cora teaching about topic sentences and thesis statements and works-cited pages, the job had just vanished. There weren't enough students for the regular faculty, and any oddjobbers or adjunct instructors had to move on.

But she hadn't moved on. She liked the small town, and how she earned her rent had become unimportant to her. And she loved the woods that crept up to the town's edge, walking through them, the rhythms of another drama she would never write rattling around in her head or, on the best days, coursing through her veins. So for the last ten months she'd waited tables down by the courthouse, sometimes taking orders from her former students, who were invariably polite and asked if she was still writing plays.

But she wasn't writing plays or sending scripts off to contests and theater festivals, not like she used to when she was in graduate school or teaching. Something had faded inside her, something that had once urged her to create, to write, to invent characters and situations—it had gone and she worried it would never come back. Not that she didn't try, sitting down at her typewriter in the mornings before work, tapping out a few lines of dialogue or sketching out rough scenes or situations in her notebook, all of them flat or boring versions of plays she'd already written in graduate school for the little black box theater, where they had received such praise from her professors.

Whether she waited tables or taught or tried to write—one thing she knew about herself was this: she had, no matter what else, an intricate mind. Where some people—her former colleagues talking noisily at the long table by the café's entrance—could discuss a story's context or articulate the theoretical apparatus that rendered a poet irrelevant and the social forces behind the work's construction all-important, she could feel, even if she could no longer write, the literary work itself, the deep, inarticulable motions of the human mind that made great literature possible, the vast polyvalent forces of thought at work in the stories of O'Connor, Gogol, Welty, in the plays of Shaw or Williams. She could feel it and she once could create it—even if on a level vastly below what seemed in other great writers second nature.

For three months she'd had a boyfriend. But what had seemed romantic had quickly become something closer to a friendship, and then acquaintanceship. And when he'd fallen asleep in the dinghy, then drifted to shore—well, standing there in the hospital cafeteria, in the overflow room, she'd looked down on him with a kind of far-off pity and horror.

Had she even known him? She didn't think so. And now here he was, red-faced and unwakeable.

+

There was another reason she stayed. She did not want to go home. She couldn't go home. She was too ashamed.

I will tell you what happened: Cora had an older sister who lived outside Omaha. As girls, they had been very close, and very different from each other. Susan was never good at school, was plump and agreeable and friendly and, while Cora was still in high school, Susan married a much older man, a man who kept horses at a little camp, horses he would rent out to anyone who wanted to ride down the trails and along the riverbank. Richard taught horseback riding to girls from town and stabled horses for those who didn't have stables. It was a good business, he was a kind man, and Susan settled in with him.

Cora had liked Richard immediately, though he was almost her father's age. He was gentle and quiet, a widower, with large capable hands. He smoked a pipe and ate apples, cores and all, and made jokes so bad Cora winced, and when she came to stay with them for the summer after she finished her graduate degree—a summer of low prospects before the sudden, last-minute offer of a job in Missouri—she got to know him better. Richard was good to her sister and the three of them tended to the horses and rode into town for Shakespeare in the Park or to shop, and if she sometimes felt his eyes lingering on her longer than they should, she simply shrugged that away. Men looked at her that way sometimes, and it was almost never a problem. She was flattered.

And when several weeks into her stay he leaned forward on the sofa and kissed her on the mouth, she didn't protest at all, but kissed him back. It was exciting being kissed by this man, this man who knew how to saddle a horse and fix a car and uproot old stumps, this older, competent man with a tattoo of an eagle on his biceps.

She kissed him, and then she felt his hand on her breast, squeezing and caressing, the tingle moving through her body. She felt him unbutton her blouse, one button, then another. Three buttons. And her hand, too, on him, lower.

And then the kiss ended and she stood up abruptly.

"I'm sorry," he said. "You're just so—"

"No, I'm sorry," she said. "I'm not—" And then she backed away from him, disheveled on the sofa. She wiped the hair from her eyes and he looked at her longingly.

Down the hall, the bathroom door opened, then closed. Her

sister had been in the shower, but now she was out. “Hello?” Susan said from the doorway and then she walked in the room, fresh and clean, wrapped in her bathrobe. “Everything OK?” she said, then sensing that it was not, she said, “What’s up?”

Cora had played the next bit over and over in her mind. She had done the wrong thing; she always did it all wrong. Instead of smiling right through it—instead of saying, “Oh, nothing, I was just going to bed”—she did what she always did in a bad situation. She froze.

“What’s going on?” her sister said, noticing now Cora’s rumpled hair, the unbuttoned blouse. “What the hell is going on?” she said.

And Cora just walked out of the room without saying anything at all.

She paced back and forth in the little guest room, then grabbed her cigarettes and a bottle of scotch from her dresser drawer and walked outside into the cool night air. The lawn was twinkling with lightning bugs and she walked across it, then leaned her back against one of the stables and lit a cigarette and drank straight from the bottle. How did she manage to fuck this up? How could she fuck this up? She drank and smoked.

Cora could hear Susan and Richard shouting at each other inside—their voices drifted across the lawn. She couldn’t tell what they were saying, but that didn’t matter. They shouted for a while and then silence. She smoked some more, ashing her cigarette into the dry grass, and soon she was very drunk. She couldn’t bear to go back inside until she knew they were asleep. And then *she* was asleep, leaning against the stable door among the hay and old boards.

It was the heat that woke her, her cigarette having set a pile of hay on fire, and that fire having spread to a larger pile of wood by the side of the stable. She stood, drunk and wavering, and because what else could she do, she shouted for help, she shouted and shouted, the flames licking up around the woodpile and threatening the stable itself.

Then she saw Richard in his bathrobe dragging the hose across the lawn—it would have been almost comic if she hadn't been so ashamed and so drunk. Reeling, actually.

The next morning Susan had said, "I think you'd better go," and Cora had agreed. One side of the stable had been charred, had been half destroyed. Richard was outside somewhere with the horses, which were still spooked from the smoke and excitement.

Cora wanted to say it hadn't been her fault, it had been *his* fault, but she couldn't figure out how to say it.

"I think it would be best if you didn't come back."

+

Still, Cora would not like to be portrayed here as a sad person. So I will tell you now that she was not sad. She was *incomplete*. And when she felt particularly incomplete, she'd walk the narrow stairs down from her apartment near the university and right into one of the bars whose jukeboxes throbbed through her bedroom floor most nights. She looked good in Jordache and a jean jacket and was skilled at a variety of billiards called Belizean that, at the time, was being played all over town. And if now and then she invited someone she met in the bar up to her apartment after the bar closed, well, that was her business and no one else seemed to care much. She wasn't, after all, from there. And she'd be leaving eventually, if she ever made a success out of writing, when the right teaching job opened up somewhere else, when she got sick of being where she was.

When she laughed, she laughed loudly. When she talked, she tended to take on the accent of the person she was speaking with, and to make her own vocabulary unthreatening. When she focused on the combination shot that would send the three ball into the side pocket, she could block out all the noise of the bar. And when she met a man she liked, she made sure he knew it, without letting him know she knew he knew it. It was a complicated business, being entirely alone in a small town and twenty-four years old, trying to explain herself to herself.

+

When the Sinaloan condition—when *the sleeps*—got bad, Cora was quick to try Eight Track, which she swallowed, then washed back with Chablis. Eight scrubbed away the flickering lights at her eye-corners and, while everyone else in the bar fell asleep, she became merely woozy, steadying herself on the pool table, shaking her head back and forth to clear away the blackness. And then a peculiar sensation of being in two places at once, of simultaneity, a feeling that seemed to increase with each dose. But when that passed, she'd blink, wipe away the ensuing, inevitable headache, and look around her.

The bartender was nowhere. She supposed he had a little cot behind the bar and had probably settled into it the moment he sensed that another sleep was coming.

Who could hear the far-off warning sirens in the noisy bar? She could, because she always paid attention, but so many were taken entirely by surprise, tilted forward in their chairs, faces pressed into pools of beer at their tables. One waitress lay on the floor surrounded by spilled hot wings, one shoe on, the other, inexplicably, fifteen feet away. The bar was entirely still, except for REO Speedwagon blaring from the jukebox.

Could she have robbed them all blind? She could have, yes. Yes, she could. But she didn't. She just waited for them to wake up, the Eight coursing through her veins, making her fingers move back and forth and her shoulders tighten and her head throb. For nearly three minutes she sat awake in the bar full of sleepers, and then, one by one, they began to wake, to rise from the floor and squeeze the beer from their T-shirts, to rub what would soon bruise, to laugh and look around nervously lest someone fail to rise. But no one did. Everyone was just fine. She was fine. She was not going to end up in an overflow ward, which is why she depended on her friend Jake, who might well have been in love with her, for her supply of Eight.

+

Once Jake told her about Eight Track, Cora always had some with her, one greenish-yellow tablet in her jean-jacket pocket and another in her purse, in case she wasn't wearing her jean jacket. It mattered little to her that she didn't know what was in it. She'd heard it was made from cold medicines and cells harvested from field mice and the distillation of exotic purple flowers that grew only in deserts, but she didn't know if any of that was true. She didn't know who made it, or how it got into those tablets and the tablets into clear plastic wrappers, exactly like the after-dinner mint wrappers at the Holiday Inn. It didn't bother her too much that she had a headache after she took the pill and then invariably stayed up half the night unsuccessfully trying to avoid the strange, vivid dreams that always came with it.

Jake told her, "Better just to take the sleep when it hits you. Eight'll split your brain in two. I'm not shitting you. I read about it somewhere," but nothing was more frightening to Cora than the possibility of never waking up. This fear only grew as the overflow rooms overflowed and people began talking about just letting the sleepers starve, or, in more sympathetic tones, administering a painless euthanasia, like they were considering in Sweden, where things were even worse.

There were drugs that would make one just slip away. . . .

+

She had written a scene in which a pool ball jumped from the pool table, rolled noisily across a bar floor, and right out the door, where it came to a rest in the gutter. It was a metaphor for something, but she wasn't sure what. Maybe her life.

She wasn't really dating Jake, but she wasn't not-dating Jake, either. Jake hung around a lot, more than was probably good, and she knew he was a little infatuated. She did nothing to put an end to that, though she didn't exactly invite it, either.

He was tall, a little overweight, softspoken in a way that seemed like gentleness. "Hey, moon girl," he'd say to her, though she could never figure out why he called her that. Was it her blue T-shirt with the crescent moons on it? Was it one of her plays, which he had read sitting cross-legged on her living room floor, the play that took place in a dying moon colony? "Hey, moon girl, what's happening?" And Cora would smile at him and they'd shoot a game of Belizean pool or walk down West Pine Street toward the woods. Jake lived on the edge of town in the family house with his older sister and her husband and six cats, so they almost never went there.

But they'd hang about in the bars or sit outside the United Dairy Farmers flicking cigarette butts into the gutter, talking about movies and bands and sometimes deeper subjects, like their futures or their parents or poetry. The sodium lights glittered on the hoods of cars. Abandoned cats slipped across the street as quickly and silently as passing thoughts.

Or they'd wind up in Cora's apartment above the throbbing bars.

Jake had a tattoo of a dagger on one shoulder and a tattoo of a guitar on fire on the other, and his dyed mop of hair looked especially black against his pale, moonlike face and pink, wet lips. He was not a handsome guy and he was two years younger than she, but he talked a good game, knew all the directors of all the movies, knew every band of any interest: Public Image Ltd and Siouxsie and the Banshees and the Psychedelic Furs. And when Cora told him about her fears, he got her the Eight Track and told her he could get more if she needed it, though the price was going up and she shouldn't take it every time, just now and then.

"But where do you get it?" she asked once.

"Guy I know name of Jimbo," he said. "I don't know where he gets it."

"And he just gives it to you?"

Jake laughed. "No, of course not. He lends me lots of stuff on consignment and I have a few clients here and there with money. They buy this or that. This or that. And I keep a pretty good cut. Good enough so I don't have to wait tables, anyway."

"What's 'this or that,'" she said, smiling, almost teasing. They were sitting on the hood of his Datsun. It was late at night. The Amtrak had just rumbled past, slowing for the station downtown. The lit windows looked ghostly, each a little diorama, each a little drama, a little dream. She'd read a poem about that once, passing windows like a passing life. Another that compared the windows on a train to ice cubes.

Such a dreamy night. And Jake laughed uncomfortably, shifted his bulk on the car's hood.

"You know," he said. "It's commerce. It's all commerce, moon girl. Every truck that passes through, every train. It's goods. I'm just a little part of that."

The moonlight caught his teeth just right, and she put her hand on his hand.

"That train that just passed?" she said. "It wasn't commerce. It was *people*."

"People who paid for tickets."

Another train was coming, but it was still far, far away, its single bright white light glimmering and tiny in the humid distance.

"What else do you sell for Jimbo?" she asked him.

"This or that," he said. "This or that. This or that."

+

She had taken an afternoon off. She had been wishing she could call her sister and just *talk*, just talk it through, but her sister almost never answered. When she did answer, she sounded cold and distant and formal, though it had been nearly two years now.

The antique mall off West Pine was quiet and cavernous, one little stall after another. Cora fingered the Fiestaware teacups and a tin stereo viewer, and then one of the sales clerks asked if she could be of help. The clerk was white-haired, thin, and nervous and she watched Cora through thick glasses. "No, I'm just looking around," Cora said, settling a snow globe back on a shelf beside a pair of brass bookends shaped like spaniels.

The woman nodded, but she didn't move.

"What?" Cora said.

The woman just stood there looking at her, and Cora flushed.

"Are you going to pay for the letter opener?" the woman asked.

Cora flushed more deeply. "What letter opener?" she asked, feeling the old bronze letter opener burning a hole in her purse. She hadn't meant to steal it. She'd meant to buy it, but at the last moment something had come over her—a presence, a feeling that at any moment the world for her could end—and she'd slipped it into her purse. It was shaped like a crane, the blade coming together at the crane's long legs. She liked that.

"I don't care," the woman was saying, "if you put the letter opener in your purse or you hold it in your hand, but when you leave the store, you will pay for it."

Cora mumbled something and turned away, and just as she did she could hear the distant sirens again, the first time in over a month. She fumbled in her purse, pushing the letter opener aside, and found the Eight.

The old woman had backed away now, having heard the sirens

too, and Cora quickly swallowed the pill dry. The old Seth Thomas clocks ticked on the walls, a row of them. The store grew silent and Cora waited three, four minutes among the knickknacks before she felt the simultaneous tug of sleep and glitter of wakefulness that meant both the Eight and the sickness were at work.

Her head hurt. She stood among the old postcards and, at the same time, by an enormous antique desk three stalls away. And in the street in front of the antique mall, among the glittering cars. And strangely somewhere far away, in a field, evening coming on and fireflies winking over the cut grass.

She was simultaneous again and dizzy as the Eight pulsed through her veins, and then the feeling faded and she resolved herself beside the counter and the cash register, in one place again.

The old woman lay on her back on a little cot behind the counter. She looked so peaceful, lost in sleep, her badly rouged cheeks sunken, her glasses a little askew.

Cora's head tingled and sparked.

She fished the letter opener from her purse and placed it carefully on the woman's chest and slipped out into the silent glare of sunlight.

The sleep lasted six minutes this time, the longest yet.

+

Eight Track was illegal. The risks, the television said, were too great. Better to sleep and then wake up healthy and sane than to risk damage—not just to the liver and the heart, but to the intricate circuitry of the mind. "It's not worth it" went the tag line, but as the sleeps persisted, so too did Eight, which only grew more expensive. And harder to find.

Jake always had a pill or two for Cora, though, so she had a little more than half a bottle full, though he never took any himself.

"I'm punk rock that way," he'd say, laughing, his doughy face and pink little mouth both appealing and repulsive.

So when Jake failed to appear at the Town Tavern one night, and then didn't call her the next day, Cora walked over to his house, but he wasn't there. Karen, his sister, hadn't seen him all day, but that wasn't unusual.

So Cora walked to the bars on West Pine Street, to the library, to the high school, then to the woods behind the high school where they sometimes went to drink. She found him there, half in and half out of his gray Datsun, parked among the weeds by the creek.

By now everyone knew someone who hadn't woken up—a neighbor, a cousin in Jeff City, that old lady who lived alone in the little cottage by the train tracks. Now Cora knew two. She stared at Jake a long time and felt herself shudder. She touched his hair. She thought maybe she'd steeled herself well enough through these many months of the sleeps, but she had not.

She knew better than to try to wake him. She wiped the little stream of drool from his cheek and righted him in his car. She brushed his black hair out of his eyes and fished his cigarettes out of his pocket. She lit one and sat in the passenger seat beside him and smoked. A squirrel walked across the power line, upsetting a row of sparrows. From the highway came the long low sounds of eighteen-wheelers. She lit another cigarette. The stream moved noiselessly, a cardboard cup slipping past. She squeezed Jake's hand. It felt warm and plump and soft.

He had been a good man. He was a good man.

She told herself that when she got home she would call the city. Then they would do whatever they did with the sleeping, take him away. But when she unlocked her apartment door she couldn't make the call. The phone lay on the floor by her futon like a sleeping black cat. She sat rigidly on the edge of the mattress and stared at it. She couldn't leave him asleep in his Datsun for another night. But she couldn't stand to make the call, either.

Who knew where they would take him?

+

The sleepers no longer overwhelmed the little regional hospital out on Highway 13, and beds no longer spilled into hallways and lobbies. The hospital was quiet again, doctors and nurses and orderlies walking briskly from room to room, the cafeteria returned to its original purpose. The sleepers were no longer their responsibility.

Now, when someone couldn't wake up, a brightly painted green-and-yellow van pulled up and two young men would slip inside discreetly and remove the sleeper. They wore bright yellow uniforms and offered condolences and hope and Yes, they said, Yes, our job is to transport your loved one to the regional facility, that is all. We are only drivers, yes. A glorified taxi service, if you like, but it costs you nothing. Yes, we're very sorry and yes, the best care will be taken, the best therapies will be applied. Doctors are working around the clock, yes, around the clock, and the day we have a successful treatment will be a relief for all of us, a thing to rejoice about. Now if you could confirm this information, if you could sign here and here and here. . . . Then they'd slide the sleeper neatly into one of several bunks in the gleaming van and carefully pull from the driveway into the street.

Then the neighbors would call one another. Sleepmobile came by for the Olpins, yes. I saw it, too. Pulled right up. But I couldn't tell which of them didn't wake up. Was it the daughter? It was the daughter. Well, that's a shame. She's a pretty thing.

Cora imagined long warehouses of sleeping people on low cots, each of them intubated, sunlit glittering bags of liquid dangling from poles. Silent nurses with white hats slipped from one bedside to another. Fluorescent light also spilled from the ceiling. No one spoke. In her imagination, it was quiet and vast. When the camera in her mind panned around, the rows of beds went on and on.

+

She didn't call the Sleepmobile; she couldn't. But she would.

On TV was a show about lions, then something about a child who could move objects simply by thinking about them. The blond little girl squeezed her eyes shut and concentrated. The camera shook and then the locked door that held her captive seemed to explode outward and she was free. On another channel, a show about how to keep broccoli crisp and tasty. Months ago, news of the sickness had turned either upbeat or vanished completely. In its place, reruns of sitcoms, local news, sports, more reruns. Movies from years ago. People hoped for a cure, or allowed the possible futility of their hopes to seep in so gradually that, really, they didn't much feel it at all. Always there was a slight risk, and always the risk increased slightly—and who could feel so imperceptible an increase from one day to the next?

She had a half bottle of Eight and that was it. A half bottle of tabs in crinkly clear plastic. She had no idea how to get more, so in desperation and fear she drove back to the high school.

Jake's body was still slumped against his steering wheel in the darkness. His hand was warm, but his breathing felt a little shallow. She would call them, she would have him whisked away to wherever they go, she knew she had to do it. He would die out here if she didn't call them.

But now she checked his jacket, searched through the glove compartment, and reached into his pants pockets, where she found both a little plastic bag with two tablets of Eight and his wallet, which contained three twenty-dollar bills and a condom. She pocketed the tablets and the bills. She would pay him back if she ever saw him again.

The lights from the soccer field beyond the woods lit his black hair. His head was pressed against the steering wheel. She touched his hair, smoothed it, then she got out of the car. She walked around to the driver's side, opened the door, and as best she could, pulled him from the seat onto the grass, where she lay him on his back, face to the stars. It was a beautiful night, cool and pleasant and lightning bugs glimmered by the side of the creek. For a little while, she lay beside him, looking up at the stars. An airplane slid slowly across the sky, blinking, blinking.

Then she smoothed his jacket, kissed him lightly on the forehead, got into his car, and drove quietly away.

+

"Why don't they just let them sleep at home?" she asked her friend Cynthia. Cynthia was cleaning the tread of her running shoes with a stick, dipping it into a cup of water, then scrubbing, then dipping it in the water.

"They need treatment," Cynthia said. "You can't treat them at home. They need professional treatment."

Cora nodded. She felt Jake's car key in her pocket. She'd have to be careful about the car in case his sister saw her driving it. For now, anyone could have stolen it. "But, I mean, I could look after a sleeping person," she said. "And those bags of fluid—"

"Nutriments," said Cynthia.

"Nutriments. I think most anyone could change those bags."

"Well, they need to be turned, there are all kinds of bodily functions and complexities."

They were sitting on the basketball court behind the high school, not far from where Cora had found Jake the week before. A little girl was trying to throw a tennis ball into the hoop, but it bounced off the backboard then rolled into the grass.

"And if everyone was having to spend their days looking after a sleeper, how'd anyone get work done is another thing," Cynthia said.

At last her shoe was clean and she slipped it on her foot and tied it. Cora didn't understand how she could be so casual about it. Cynthia's own aunt had been whisked away a couple months ago, but here she was in her clean running shoes looking up at the gray sky. The leaves were just beginning to change.

"You going to visit your aunt?" Cora asked.

"Not sure if I see the point, since she won't know I'm there."

"You know where they're keeping her?"

Cynthia lay back on the court and shielded her eyes with her hand. "They left an address with my uncle. Somewhere outside Kansas City, I think."

"So you're not going to visit?"

Her friend just stared at the sky.

"I mean, aren't you scared?"

"Goddammit," Cynthia said quietly, almost to herself. "Can you leave it alone?"

3 GLASS & CORA

Sometimes the older kids parked their pickup trucks in a circle in the BI-LO parking lot, headlights facing out. That way, they could sit on the tailgates and drink and talk and smoke. They had a boom box and the low beat carried across the asphalt all the way to the street. Glass had seen them there back when his father drove him and Scooby home from the movies, their bright silhouettes, the parking lot vast and black and empty, the ring of glowing headlights like a flying saucer. He wondered what they talked about, the older boys.

They wouldn't include him, he was sure, not even when he *was* older. They were the tough kids, the boys whose fathers drove trucks, whose mothers worked for John Bee Uniforms Inc., the shopkeepers' kids. They were the same ones who sat on the wall outside the high school smoking cigarettes and laughing, girls leaning heavily against them, girls with pink lip gloss and perfect even little white teeth like Chiclets chewing gum, wearing black T-shirts: Stevie Nicks, Cheap Trick, .38 Special. They were terrifying and intriguing at once.

Early one Saturday morning, Glass bicycled from his house to the BI-LO and found their beer bottles, their cigarette butts, a discarded cassette tape, its shiny brown ribbon pulled from the case as if it were an eviscerated animal.

In *The Mirovac Chronicles* all the kids—all the tough kids, the nerdy kids, the awkward and angry and rash—all of them ascended under thought control toward evenness, toward acceptability. They wore bright green polo shirts or pastel jackets or penny loafers, they got to school on time, they sat in even rows and raised their hands when they knew the answers. The adults praised them, and they smiled and said they'd seen things fresh, had come to understand the world anew.

"Those guys are losers," Scooby told him once when Glass brought up the tailgaters.

"Yeah," said Glass.

"And they're assholes, too."

This was before people began falling asleep in a big way. They were lying on the floor in Scooby's living room, a board game they'd abandoned midway through before them, the TV on. *Sanford and Son*.

"And they're not even that badass."

Glass nodded, holding a game piece up to the light, a little plastic goblin, turning it so he caught its silhouette. When he squinted, he thought it might even look threatening.

"You wanna see something badass?" Scooby was saying.

"Sure."

Scooby scrambled to his feet and disappeared into the back room. On the television, a commercial for Doan's Pills. "Oh, my aching back," said the housewife, putting down her mop and leaning painfully against her kitchen counter. Glass set the plastic goblin down on the game board.

When Scooby returned, he was carrying a brown paper lunch bag. He reached inside and then was holding a small black pistol, turning it over and over in his hands.

It looked cold and heavy. It looked angry.

"Where'd you find that?"

"It's my dad's. He keeps it inside one of his boots."

The woman on TV was still talking about those pills. They'd played the commercial twice in a row.

"Can I hold it?"

+

The sleeper facilities had been constructed hastily and stood like long gray warehouses on the edges of Kansas City and Springfield. On their rooftops, giant air conditioners rumbled and hummed. Behind the front door, two receptionists always sat at marble counters. They were tired, but cheerful. To be cheerful was a large part of their job.

"The very best care," said the men who drove the green-and-yellow vans, who transported Glass's father to Kansas City from the hospital one day in October. Glass had stood by while they wheeled him and several of the other sleepers to their van, loaded them on the fold-down sleeping shelves, and drove quietly away. Glass watched that van glide down MacGregor Street, over the little hill, until at last it vanished.

Shane said, "I guess we'd best get going," and Glass nodded.

When they'd detached one of the feeding tubes from his father's arm, Glass had noticed the coin-size, perfectly round purple bruise the needle had left behind. That image stayed with him.

A purple moon.

+

Glass visited his father once at the Kansas City facility. The receptionist had asked Shane for Olaf's name, social security number or date of birth, and then located him, level B, aisle 14, bed 12.

"Like baseball tickets," Shane had said under his breath.

They'd taken the stairs, then followed the aisle numbers, which were painted on the walls. The air was heavy and still. A woman was pushing a little cart loaded with glittering bags of fluid down the aisle next to them. The cart rattled and the bags wobbled, catching and winking in the light. Across the room another woman was struggling with an IV, gently slapping a sleeping young man's arm to raise a vein. Next to his father's bed, another was efficiently shaving a sleeper's growth of beard with an electric razor.

His father's face was shiny and pink, as if too much fluid had been allowed to drain into him. He looked, Glass thought, puffy. When Glass touched his hand, he found it also warm and swollen. His father's eyelids pulsed for a moment, then twitched. His eyebrows were overgrown and gray.

"I don't want to come here again," he said to Shane.

The nurse went on shaving the sleeper in the next bed. When she finished, she tucked the electric razor into the pocket of her white coat.

"You sure?" Shane asked.

At this point, his father had been asleep for a year.

+

Once, Glass caught sight of Cora through the window of Java Junction. She was sitting at a high table reading from a thin book, underlining something. At first he winced, the memory of Scooby lying lifelessly on the muddy riverbank filling his mind again, that feeling of helplessness and defeat. But then he began to observe her. She was lost in thought. It looked like she was reading a script, but Glass wasn't sure about that. She wore a black T-shirt and pale blue acid-washed jeans and had a red bandana tied around her head. Her hand that held the pencil was beautiful, pale, with long fingers. Her fingernails were painted black. She sipped her coffee, then, after another moment, looked up, right at him.

Glass flushed and held up his hand, a kind of wave. Then he walked briskly away, embarrassed, as if he'd been caught spying.

After she'd saved Scooby's life, Scooby had lain on that riverbank panting. He wouldn't stop panting, as if he couldn't get enough air. Glass tried to stop crying and at first he couldn't, but then he swallowed hard. After a minute, Scooby sat up. "My chest hurts," he said, still panting, and Cora laughed, exhausted and relieved and soaking wet. "I'm glad that's the worst of it," she said, "because I thought you were gonna die."

And then the three of them sat there in silence for a minute, the sun sprinkling down on them through the trees. "That your beer?" she asked the boys, gesturing upriver to where the rest of the string of beer cans was entangled in branches at the riverbank.

"Yeah," Glass said. "We found them."

"OK," she said. "Well, I can see it was starting out to be a pretty fine day for you two."

Glass nodded. He didn't know what to say. He had the feeling he was in trouble again.

"You OK?" she asked Scooby for a third time, and Scooby said he was, that his chest hurt was all, and then they were in a gray Datsun, Scooby in the front seat and Glass in the back, his soaking-wet shorts sticking to the vinyl seat.

"I won't tell," she said, smiling conspiratorially.

Glass remembered all of this as he jogged down West Pine away from her.

+

There she had been, sitting in the coffee shop. Right there, drinking coffee, her long, beautiful fingers wrapped around the hot coffee mug, the startled expression on her face when she saw him through the window. And what a fool he had been to hold out his hand like that, in that motionless wave like he'd seen the tough guys do in the movies. And how he'd turned coward and jogged away, past the antique mall and the courthouse and the stupid statue of Daniel Boone on the courthouse lawn.

Shane had made chicken pot pies—the frozen kind that Glass liked more than almost anything—and Glass had struggled to finish his, and Shane said, "You seem awfully somber, Charles," which was Glass's real name, the name no one called him, and Glass had said he was just fine, he had a lot of homework, could he be excused to do his homework?

"He doesn't have homework," Carlos said. "Tomorrow's a field trip."

"Sure," Shane said, looking at Glass curiously, then dumping the empty tinfoil containers in the garbage. "Sure thing. Go do your homework."

+

He felt his father's presence beside him vividly. He could smell him in the darkening evening: Copenhagen snuff and breath mints.

Now the scene shifted, the lights above the little living room blackened, the set turned and the room slid silently away.

Steam rose from the stage, lit red and blue, an outdoor light. Prop brambles and thicket, hooked like barbed wire. A dilapidated yellow farmhouse painted on a scrim, behind it a vast cornfield. Glass sensed that the stage extended infinitely back, back, back, into a blood-lit farmscape, strange and fallow and apocalyptic.

But in the foreground, an actual minibus, brightly painted in pinks and greens, graffitied over with black scrawls, a minibus, its headlights lighting the stage.

And in the headlights' glare, the boy was crying, was wiping away tears with his jacket sleeve while the young woman stood beside him. "It's all right," she was saying, "we'll go home when it's safe. When it's safe, we'll drive right back home."

But the boy kept crying, there in the headlights. He didn't want to go any farther, and his despair enveloped Glass.

And when Glass's eyes drifted over the stage, when they drifted to the minibus, he could just discern another figure, a dark figure crouched on the minibus's roof, a figure with great black trembling wings, a shifting body, crouched and coiled. And then it was flexing those wings—

When Glass woke up, he could tell that it was very late. The sickness had come and gone in the middle of the night, interrupting a dreamless sleep with a vivid dream.

+

On Easter Sunday his father would hide chocolate eggs around the house and out on the patio and even in the yard. One hundred little chocolate eggs wrapped in gold, pink, green, blue foil that glittered in the light. When Glass woke, his father would hand him a plastic beach pail and tell him, "Have at it, Charles."

Chocolate eggs in the row of cactus plants on the windowsill, among the wine bottles in the low kitchen cabinet, in the saucepans and drinking glasses. He'd hidden them in the medicine cabinet among the BandAids and among the worn-out towels in the linen closet. And Glass gathered them, always looking for the one plastic egg his father included among the chocolates, a hollow egg, a special egg.

In 1982, when Glass was only ten years old, a year before the Sinaloan event, winter lingered. Frost laced the grass outside and crunched under his feet as he gathered eggs from the garden and dropped them in the yellow plastic pail. But he could not find the hollow egg, the one that had the present in it, the movie tickets, the two five-dollar bills, the ancient Roman coins. He'd searched and searched, moving inside and out through the sliding-glass doors. He'd looked among the boxes of bones in the basement, around the gleaming lab equipment, in the skulls' eyeholes, then gone back out onto the deck in the cold, his father closing the sliding-glass door behind him to keep the house warm.

His face hurt from the cold and he could see his breath. The pail was wrist-deep in chocolate eggs, and his father sat on the sofa inside, smiling, reading a book. Glass searched among the trowels, inside the little hurricane lamp, and then he spotted it, it was right there, plain as day, in the middle of the ice-crusted birdbath. How had he missed it?

He ran to it—this year it was pale green plastic and heavy and when he twisted it open, a plastic wristwatch fell into his palm, a Swatch, green and yellow with crazy, multicolored hands.

"I found it!" he shouted, running from the birdbath up the steps to the deck, running to the sliding-glass door, and then he felt the impact of the glass door hard on his face, felt and heard it shatter at once, time slowing down for him, his father slowly lowering his book and turning his head as Glass crashed through the glass and the glass slid down like guillotine blades around him, cutting into his cheek, his thigh, and his father on his feet now as Glass fell forward into the room.

The feeling of blood sliding down his cheek, tickling his ear, wetting his hair, his father on the telephone as Glass lay among shards, looking at the ceiling, afraid to touch his own face.

And then his father kneeling beside him, pressing dish towels against the cuts on his face, more blood pooling around his ankles.

The doctor stitched up his cheek, his forehead, his wrist, his thigh, and Glass whimpered. "You're pretty lucky," she said, bending over him, smelling of perfume and cigarettes—lucky it had been a cold day, lucky he had been wearing his heavy down coat. "You're a lucky guy," she said again, examining the stitches.

His father drove him home and then poured himself a drink. Broken glass decorated the beige carpet. "Let's not do that again," his father told him after he'd finished a couple drinks. He was on his knees, picking up the shards, then scrubbing the dried blood out of the carpet.

Glass didn't answer. He turned the plastic Swatch over and over in his hands.

"Damn," the kids at school said the next day, examining the bandages across his face beneath which the stitches tingled, stitches that would eventually become one long, straight, pink scar on his left cheek and another above his eye. Smaller ones on his chest. "What happened?"

"Glass," said Glass.

"Glass?"

"Yeah. I cut myself on some glass."

"No way."

"Yeah. Walked through a glass door."

The kids stared at him strangely, and Glass felt the tan threads that held his wounds together tugging on his skin.

Silence. Then, "Did it hurt?" one of them asked.

"I don't even really remember," he said. "I don't think so."

"Damn." One of them ran his fingers gently over the bandages above his eye. "Damn. You can feel the stitches through the bandage. How many stitches?"

"A lot," he said.

In this way, he earned the name Glass.

+

He watched Cora pull her little gray Datsun into the parking lot across from the Tea Haus and then he watched her get out and look to the left and right, as if to make sure no one was watching her. Glass lingered on the other side of the street, pretending to look at a pair of bright blue tennis shoes in the shop window.

When she walked down Maguire Street, though, Glass followed her. When she ran into a couple of friends—a young woman and a skinny guy with a beard and long hair, someone his father would have called "a damned hippie"—he lingered again, pretending to tie his shoe, then looking at his Swatch.

When she turned the corner, Glass followed, and when she entered the pharmacy, Glass sat on a bench two stores down.

He noticed everything about her. She was dressed nicely, a black skirt and a dark blue top with a silver necklace shaped like a starburst. Red high-tops. When she exited the pharmacy carrying a white paper bag, he followed her again, down the block to the Black Walnut Pub. When she didn't emerge after ten minutes, he looked nonchalantly through the window.

There she was. She was waiting tables.

+

"She's a waitress," he told Scooby, who was seated uncomfortably atop the bike rack outside the school.

"Whatever," said Scooby. He didn't like to think about the day he almost drowned. It embarrassed him. But Glass kept bringing up that woman.

"I saw her in the coffee shop, too. And in the library."

"Uh-huh."

"Aren't you even curious? I thought you'd be curious."

"Damn, Glass." Scooby crushed his empty can of Pepsi, then threw it as hard as he could across the parking lot. "You gotta let that *go*. You're gonna end up a stalker. You gotta let it *go*."

So Glass didn't bring it up much with Scooby. But that didn't mean he stopped thinking about her, imagining her long elegant fingers turning the pages of that script, her black concert T-shirt, her dark hair, cut severely, like a black slash across her forehead. He imagined conversations they might have, how Glass might just casually walk into the Black Walnut Pub and ask for a seat, how surprised she'd be to see him there in the corner booth, how she'd slide onto the vinyl seat beside him and ask what he was doing there.

"Just passing through," he'd say, because he had money in his pocket.

It wasn't love, exactly. Glass had never been in love. It was proximity. He wanted her to notice him. He wanted her to understand him, he wanted her to like him. And he wanted to look at her, to admire her shape, the way she bit her lower lip when she read.

All of this he wrote down in the spiral notebook that he hid under the carpet in his temporary bedroom: how he wanted to know everything about her, how he wanted to tell her about his sleeping father, his temporary father, the cat's lungs splattered on the science room floor. His mother in Minnesota, a dental hygienist, a substitute teacher, moving from job to job. But not just his problems. He wanted her to know how he and Scooby had sneaked out one evening and stolen two stop signs near Pertle Lake, wrenching them free from their posts and hiding them behind Scooby's dad's garage. Then how he'd worried that someone might crash their car, that someone might die and he'd called Scooby the next morning, and Scooby had laughed. "C'mon, man," Scooby said. "There's hardly ever any traffic there. Ain't no one gonna crash and die on those empty roads."

How he had held Scooby's dad's black pistol, the weight of it in his hands, deadly.

How there was some creep driving around outside the school throwing wadded up pornographic pictures at the kids walking home. A real creep, though Glass had flattened a couple of the pictures out and kept them between the pages of volume three of *The Microvac Chronicles*.

How Shane came home from the university smelling of something sweet, of bourbon, and relaxed on the sofa, having picked up a video at King Video, having picked up takeout Chinese at the Red Dragon.

He poured himself another drink and he and Carlos and Glass watched Chuck Norris take down drug dealers until Shane fell asleep still holding his bourbon balanced on his thigh.

All of this Glass wanted to share.

+

He was bicycling home when he saw another green-and-yellow van pull quietly from the lot behind student housing, just down the hill from the university. It idled at the light on Grover Street and Highway 13, then pulled easily away. Another sleeper. He tried to tell Shane about it, but Shane brushed it aside. Shane never wanted to talk about the sleepers. If Glass brought it up, he grew abrupt or changed the subject. Or he'd say, "Well, we all gotta go sometime, right? Hopefully later than sooner," and with that he'd be done with it.

But other people talked about sleepers all the time. Scooby's parents talked to other parents who tracked the sickness and kept notes on sleep times in other areas, who knew that across the country sleeps were growing longer and the number of those who never woke up, while still small, increased with the sleep times. And certain areas, they knew, had experienced uncommonly long sleeps, had alarming numbers who couldn't wake up.

"The news don't cover it right," Scooby's father said, "but we know pretty well what's going on." He was talking to Shane, but Shane shook his head and glanced at the boys, who were half-listening and half-watching a cartoon on TV. They were in the Franklins' living room. They had a bowl of Doritos between them.

"They might as well know," Scooby's father said, but more quietly. But Shane said nothing to that. The stakes seemed different to him—between Mr. Franklin and himself. He sipped his beer.

So awkward to sit on this man's couch knowing one of them was blessed and the other was not, and he didn't really want to talk about it, not because he couldn't keep his resentment hidden, but because it embarrassed him that it ran so deep. So he drank again, and soon had too much.

But Mr. Franklin, Shane, and most people in town got along as they always had, at least outwardly—they did their jobs and came home to their families, they shopped and made dinner and ate out on weekends. If anything, they were kinder to one another than they used to be, at least outwardly, at least in public, at least most of the time. They kept one another informed. "I heard the sickness hit pretty hard a couple weeks ago in Jones County," someone said. "I heard so-and-so's mother didn't wake up, though it might be a blessing, her being so old." I heard, I heard.

"What if this goes on forever?" someone said, to which her friend shook her head. "Ain't nothing like this go on forever. They working on it." Meaning the scientists. Not the politicians. The politicians never did anything right. It was the politicians who were keeping the news from reaching anyone, who were making it hard to know what was going on in Cleveland, in St. Louis, in Miami, much less in Denmark or the rest of the world.

But the faucet hadn't been turned off completely. Rather, the focus had changed from the seemingly endless, the forgettable, the dreary number of sleeps to the progress that was being made in the laboratories and the universities and pharmaceutical companies, the small successes, the imagined successes, the reasons for hope.

"They might as well know," Scooby's father said again.

+

Carlos buried himself deeper into his wasps. He had captured several and kept them in an aquarium on top of which he'd attached a mesh screen. He fed them liver and closely monitored their interactions. "The dark brown one," he told Glass, "is dominant. When he's on the liver, the others stay back. But when he's done, that one with the gold fleck on her abdomen gets to eat. Then the light brown one. He's a dirt dauber, not actually a wasp. One after the other, in order, just like dogs."

Glass peered into the aquarium, which Carlos had landscaped with a plastic castle and a few Matchbox cars and a model airplane. The black wasps rose and fell, they bumped stupidly into the screen ceiling, they crawled over the model airplane and the castle, their spurred front legs groping, groping. They were like sad, lost men, Glass thought.

+

Cora had seen Glass following her but didn't take it too seriously. Grown men followed her occasionally, so why shouldn't a boy?

The grown men worried her sometimes—since the sleeps began, they'd become more frequent and friendly and persistent, and she'd gotten adept at losing them, at brushing them off. At work, they made flirtatious remarks. It didn't matter if she dressed formally, if she did her best to create a distance, to smile professionally. "Yeah, *you* can take my order," one of them had just told her, laughing, and she stood there in silence, holding her little order pad, staring right at him until he settled down and ordered the spaghetti plate.

But Glass was different. He looked to be about eleven years old, a little awkward, a little skinny. Brown hair. He had two scars on his face, a long one on his left cheek and another over his right eye, like he'd been in a car accident. When he'd leaned forward crying that day on the riverbank, she thought she'd seen another on his neck, disappearing into his T-shirt.

He was, as her mother would have said, clearly *sweet* on her, and when she passed him on the street, she smiled and said hello, and he blushed fiercely, looked down and hurried past.

She'd been there once, too, years ago, a girl utterly sweet on an older boy she'd met at Wendy's. How she admired the way he tore the top off his pack of cigarettes so he could examine all twenty, how his nimble fingers would fish one out and slip it between his curled lips. How he'd offer her one and they'd lean against his father's Volaré, smoking and looking at the moon. That was years ago, in Omaha, and he'd eventually moved away. For a week she'd mooned dreamily about the house, though in truth she'd only spent a handful of evenings with him.

So if she saw Glass tiptoeing around in the background here and there, she understood it, and though she didn't invite it she didn't do anything to stop it, either.

+

Far more pressing concerns for Cora were the lack of Eight and what to do about Jake's gray Datsun. She'd come to depend on the Datsun but knew that Jake's sister must be wondering about it. Of course, *anyone* could have stolen it. Anyone could have come upon Jake and simply pushed him from the car and driven off. The car could be anywhere.

Still, she made a point of not driving it too much during the day and parking it in the lot behind the courthouse, where it wasn't visible to just anyone. If anyone asked, she'd say he had given her the keys. He couldn't exactly deny it, could he?

And she was down to just a half a bottle of Eight—the twelve tablets she had when Jake fell asleep plus the two she'd found in his jean jacket pocket, minus the three she'd had to take. That was it. It might last a year if she was lucky. After that, she'd be like anyone else, head to the dashboard.

She'd asked a couple of Jake's friends but they'd just shrugged. "That shit's really hard to get these days," they'd said. "Jake had a line on it, but it was drying up when he fell asleep. And seriously—

it'll fuck you up if you get too much in your system. It'll split your brain in two." And she'd nodded and said she guessed she'd just keep looking. "Good luck," Jake's friends told her.

+

No one called it The Sinaloan condition anymore. They mostly called it *the sleeps*. And as the sleeps spread, she thought more and more about her sister. She was the only family Cora had—their mother had died when she was in college and she never really had a father, not one she could look to. "I met your father on a hayride," her mother used to say, smiling. "We were both very young. It lasted a few years and thats all there is to it. He's in Italy now, last I heard." How strong her mother had been, raising Cora and Susan on a receptionist's salary, how proud she had been of Cora's athleticism, of her successes at school, how proud she had been of Susan's marriage and good sense. And now her mother was dead. And Susan wouldn't speak to her. It was all wrecked, wrecked.

At her best, Cora felt great, knocking off work and walking over to Hero's to shoot a few games of Belizean and drink. Even now, even with the sleeps coming on and on.

But at her worst, Cora longed for family, for any connection that extended beyond the next day. She remembered sitting on the curb with Jake, smoking and talking about old times, about new wave bands, TV shows and sometimes more, sometimes dreams and poetry and more and more. Now Jake was gone. She missed him. She missed having friends. And most of all, she missed having a family.

+

The green-and-yellow van that Glass watched pull from student housing: Cora saw it, too, but much farther down Grover Street, where it intersected Lamar, just before the Kmart by Highway 70.

Cora had seen six or seven of those vans since they started cart-ing the sleepers off to wherever they went, months ago. The vans made her tremble and a fog of horror would descend over her, a sense of doom, wordless and profound, a certainty about her own end and the end of everyone she knew. Then, if she wasn't working, she would walk and walk, up and down the long residential streets, past the low ranch houses and the yellow brick dormitories, along Highway 13 past the Howard Johnson's, the McDonald's, the seedy Econo Lodge, its red-and-yellow sign blinking on and off into the night. She would walk though her feet hurt from waitressing. She would walk, though her whole body hurt, up and down the aisles of Gluck Hardware, her fingers caressing the faucets, the heavy wrenches, the little row of hammers, each one a little larger than the next. Up and down the aisles of BI-LO, examining varieties of bread. The doom ticked in her chest like a clock.

Then slowly the anxiety would slip away and a new forgetfulness would come over her, a new calm. And she would light a cigarette and relax and everything would be all right again.

She had always been first rate at whatever she attempted. That was, it seemed to her, the strange thing about her present predicament, her current mediocrity—single, paid with tips, living in a town none of her friends in Omaha had ever heard of.

Back home, she had been special. She had won the statewide junior diving championship, not once, but three times. She had ranked third in her high school class only because she had taken the hardest classes, had refused to pad her average with beginning composition or art or shop. She had been pretty and bright and fun and had her picture in the newspaper several times, and when she'd matriculated to the University of Nebraska, and not Stanford, the adults she knew were happy because Nebraska had kept one of its high achievers, because Stanford had nothing on the Cornhuskers, nothing at all.

She'd captained the diving team at Nebraska and nearly led them to two Big Eight titles. She'd majored in English *and* German and graduated *summa cum laude*. So how on earth had she wound up here, in this little town in western Missouri, waiting tables at the Black Walnut Pub and walking up and down the aisles of the BI-LO?

She was thinking about this as she looked at the line of Pelikan pens at the Office Supply & Typewriter Repair. They were expensive and beautiful, green-and-blue lacquer. They reminded her of the pen her German teacher used to carry, how he'd roll it between his fingers as he lectured. The sign said they had solid gold nibs. They cost nearly fifty dollars. Yellow autumn light slipped in through the store windows. Dust suspended in the air. She could hear the proprietor, whose nametag said she was Maggie, explaining something about typewriter ribbon to a young man in a honey-colored leather jacket.

When she was certain no one was looking, she slipped one of the pens into her purse, then lingered about the store for another few minutes, pretending to look at various binders. She smiled at Maggie before walking out.

+

When she completed a perfect dive, when she felt her body slice into the water at exactly the right angle, splashlessly, it felt to her as if time passed very slowly, as if the film slowed down. She was alert to every moment as she descended. She saw her coach standing by the edge of the pool, his notepad in his hand, mouth half open. She saw the other team in their matching red diving suits and blue rubber caps. Her body turned again and again and then she stretched out and, like a knife, she entered the water.

Nothing in her life could compare to those moments, the quick thrill that slowed time so completely. But when she stole something, when she slipped that expensive Pelikan pen into her purse and walked out of the store, well, she got a taste of what she'd savored much more completely years ago. A thrill of danger and perfect execution.

This was why, when she felt the certainty of doom crowd around her, when work or writing or a good, half-drunken game of Belizean pool couldn't calm her down, this was why she sometimes, very occasionally, stole things, inconsequential things, things she didn't even necessarily want. Not often. Just now and then.

And then there had been the time she felt herself lift from the high diving board just a little wrongly, her balance not quite right, and when she tucked her body into a ball, when she felt herself slowly turning, she knew she'd gotten it wrong. It all moved so slowly, so when the back of her head smacked the diving board, hard, she wasn't surprised, not in the instant before she lost consciousness and fell splayed into the water and quickly sank to the bottom of the pool where she drifted for more than a minute by the drain, her body limp, her brain vetoed.

When she finally woke, she felt first of all the water that came gurgling up from her lungs spill over her chin and cheeks and she coughed and retched and never again had she felt such panic and fear. Maybe this was why she could not stand the sleeps, the idea that blackness might outrun her, might overtake and smother her, a blackness from which she might never emerge.

She walked slowly in the direction of her apartment. She was feeling better now. This was the kind of autumn day she loved because it reminded her of her childhood, the smell of dead leaves and mulch and the coming winter. A chill in the air, an expectation of snow. The sunlight coming in slantwise and golden and a breeze that made the flag snap high on the flagpole.

"I saw you steal that pen," Glass said to her.

+

He was standing by the mailbox on the corner, hands in his pocket. He looked nervous. He looked like he was trying not to look nervous.

She paused, about to deny it. But why should she deny it? He was a kid. A kid who was sweet on her. Pointless to deny it. It was nothing. So she didn't deny it. She felt herself smile, slowly. "Did you now?" she said. Then, after a moment, "Are you going to do something about it?"

"No," Glass said. She could tell that he was making an effort to look into her eyes, but his eyes kept darting away.

"Well, that's a relief."

"I mean, why would I tell on you?"

"I don't know. I don't exactly know you."

Glass shrugged. "I'm not like that," he said.

"You're not a narc."

"Of course not," Glass said, though he wasn't sure what a narc was. Something bad, obviously. "Not me," he said.

She kept walking, and he walked beside her. She could hear the swish-swish of his windbreaker, his arms swinging back and forth as he tried to keep up with her. He was small for his age, a little bit of a miniature, she thought: all to scale, but scaled down. His clothes were too big.

"I just wanted you to know I saw," he said after they'd walked half a block. "And I'm cool with it."

"Tell you what," she said, after another block, reaching into her purse. She handed him the pen. "Why don't you keep it. I don't really want it." She smiled as kindly as she could.

Then she climbed the steps to her little apartment above Hero's Bar. Glass turned the pen over and over in his hands. It was beautiful, blue and black and glistening, the tip shiny as a gold tooth. A fifty-dollar pen.

+

Whenever she had to take Eight Track, her head split in two. There would be two of her. One of her stood by the dresser in her bedroom observing the other of her who sat on the sofa staring at the flickering television set. It was impossible to explain, the doubleness. Her whole body tingled and burned and she would feel her brain turning on its brainstem in the black lily pond inside her skull. She was at the dresser and she was on the sofa, and all around her the populace was asleep, was asleep, was asleep.

She would stay divided in two for only a moment, half-aware and functioning—but in two places at once. In the kitchen and the bathroom. In the stairwell and on the street.

Then the effect would diminish. Her two selves would come closer and closer together, in time and space. One self would be just a few steps behind the other, then a step behind, and then they would merge and she would look out of not two pairs of eyes, but one.

And how her head hurt.

And for two nights, she would have such vivid dreams, one dream continuing languorously from the previous. She was in a park on a hot summer night. The lightning bugs rose and fell in the bushes, among the parked cars in the parking lot. Couples and families walked the paths, past the recreation center, past the restrooms and ticket booths. A beautiful summer night, a strange summer night, a sense of apprehension and near disaster, though only she seemed to notice or feel it.

She'd walk the paths, paths in a strange park in a strange town far from anywhere she knew.

4 A BIG SLEEP

Shane drank too much. He knew it. And he knew that if he kept at it, his nose would turn red, then purple with burst blood vessels, that he'd develop a paunch and bags under his eyes. Plenty of his colleagues had turned out like that. Still, he drank too much. Not during the day. He was clear during the day. But at night, he'd pour himself one drink after another as he graded exams or flipped through the television channels or read a news magazine.

He'd thought maybe having another kid around the house—Olaf's kid—might inspire him to better behavior. But it didn't. He'd stay sober until both kids went to bed, and then he'd start pouring himself drinks. He'd read a mystery novel, but lose track of the plot after a while. Sometimes he'd wake up in the morning lying on sheets wet with the bourbon that had spilled while he lay in bed and drank. He'd quickly strip his bed and stuff the sheets in the washing machine before going groggily to wake Carlos and Glass.

Glass was nothing he'd ever wanted, though he'd told Olaf years ago that if something happened to him, he'd make sure Glass was all right. God knows his mother didn't want him. She'd made that clear.

Carlos was different. Carlos was his own son and clearly exceptional. His wasp colony had grown increasingly elaborate, one aquarium connected to another with a series of tubes that the wasps traversed clumsily, moving from invented landscape to invented landscape. In one aquarium he'd created what looked like a Dutch countryside, set with plastic windmills, wheat fields made from hundreds of yellow pipe cleaners, a toy train and a meandering tinfoil river.

Another held the surface of the moon, craters and lunar mountains Carlos had created out of cardboard covered with more tinfoil—strange vistas, a plastic moon rover. A third he called Wasp Christmas. This was perhaps the best of them, a tiny Christmas tree that blinked with various lights connected to a hidden battery pack. There were presents, two fireplaces with flickering electric flames, and a chimney constructed from Plasticine delicately engraved with bricks, tiny stockings cut from fabric. The wasps buzzed around the Christmas tree like terrifying creatures.

He soon had four, then five aquariums connected with wide plastic tubes he'd found somewhere, and the wasps built nests, groping their ways from one to the other.

Carlos monitored the sizes of their nests and fed them peaches, liver, and a substance he concocted himself. He called it "wasp nectar."

Glass was another story. He had trouble at school. He was sent home a second time when at recess two pornographic pictures fell from between the pages of a book he was reading and were then passed around among the other seventh graders.

Glass, Shane decided, was a mess. Not a bad kid, but troubled. And trouble. He was fun—usually voluble. Sometimes he talked so much Shane had to interject, to say, "Slow down, kiddo!" and Glass would catch his breath and start his story from the beginning.

+

Many years ago, Shane and Olaf had been great friends. Olaf was older. He had been Shane's mentor when Shane was an MA student, and then Shane had gone away to Kansas State to get his PhD, then returned to his alma mater as an assistant professor. He knew he had Olaf to thank for that, and the two men had grown even closer. They drank together at the Brown Derby, which was classy and served mixed drinks. Or they drank together at the VFW on the edge of town by the highway, where they were sure they wouldn't run into students. Still, Shane could never rid himself completely of the sense that he was drinking with someone who was both a good friend and his former professor, so when Olaf spoke, Shane listened. And if Shane disagreed with Olaf, he kept his disagreement mild. He loved Olaf as much as he'd ever loved any friend, and seeing him asleep—his hands puffed up and pink, his cheeks strangely shiny—well, he had been glad Glass didn't want to visit him in that condition again.

That they drank at the VFW was funny to Shane, who had never been in the military. The only war Olaf had been near was WWII, where, as a teenager, he'd spent a few miserable years in the Hitler Youth, before landing a job packing live shells into cardboard containers. His terrible eyesight, he said, probably saved him. Either that, or dumb luck.

At any rate, the two men would drink and gossip and old Doris, another German who worked behind the dingy bar, would join in. "You know," Olaf would say under his breath, his accent quite thick even after thirty years in the United States, "that old broad was once a Hamburg whore. She's a hell of a good woman now," and Shane would laugh and Doris, at the far end of the bar, would look their way and ask if they needed topping off.

The vets would come and go. They all knew Olaf and would slap him on the back and call him the Old Kraut. Most of them were farmers, or they worked in trucking, and Olaf was an oddity in their bar. And, by extension, so was Shane.

The farmers interested Olaf the most because they'd bring him the artifacts their plows turned up: scrapers and cores and projectile points and potsherds, and once a clay amulet with the image of a spider scratched into it, all of it archaic or pre-archaic or woodland era. If the artifacts were interesting, he'd head out there with his graduate students, who'd walk the plowed fields with him looking for surface finds, which they'd gather in little plastic Ziploc bags, noting details of each in spiral reporter's notebooks.

Once, Olaf had excavated a potato field of particularly rich black soil—a thousand years ago it had been a swamp—and found over three hundred footlong flint ceremonial blades and evidence of the wooden basket that had carried them before they were all sunk, a sacrifice, he said, to some god. He had written a book about it.

As Shane lay in bed reading a mystery novel, drinking scotch, only half aware of the plot, he remembered one night years ago when he and Olaf were sharing a motel room near where they were digging outside Bolivar. They'd stayed up all night in that grim beige room drinking and smoking and telling stories of malfeasance, of archaeologists who salted their sites with artifacts, who faked postholes, who stole one another's research and wives and girlfriends with such brazenness, of drunks and flunkies and secret geniuses and enormous finds made by breathtaking coincidence. The graduate students sat on the motel room floor and just listened, leaning in, ashing their cigarettes into little plastic motel cups.

And now Olaf was asleep in some facility in Kansas City. And Glass was asleep in his little bed. And Carlos was up late reading something or other, the encyclopedia maybe, a flashlight glowing under the covers.

Who could have imagined it would come to this? Not Shane, sipping his bourbon and falling drunkenly asleep with the bedside light on.

+

The wasps also slept. Every night, when the sun went down, they grew lazy and slow, stupid and half dormant, bouncing against the plastic Christmas tree or between the vast lunar mountains until they settled onto the tinfoil and plastic. They crawled blackly over the train cars, their front legs groping. Little clusters of them slept in tunnels, in papery nests.

Sometimes Glass would sit in the garage and watch them, or at night he'd try to rouse them, shining a flashlight on their shiny black bodies or tapping at the glass with a spoon. But they paid him little mind. They rose and fell over the rotting peach Carlos had left in the aquarium he called Beneath the Ocean, the one with the plastic fish and the great red Plasticine crab, claws outstretched.

Sometimes Glass wondered if the wasps would outlive him. Then, no, he thought. They are working on a cure. All the scientists in the world are working on a cure, he told himself, because that's what Mrs. Kogan had said in class. It was what most people believed—if we can just survive long enough, if we can keep waking up, waking up.

At the same time, he remembered his father on his little bed in that vast room in the sleeper facility outside Kansas City. His small, shiny body, his pink face and dried lips and hairy ears, one bed among many. All of those bodies in their own vast aquarium, the nurses pushing carts among the rows of them.

+

There had been reports of sleeps of unusual intensity in India and Ethiopia, but the newspapers, perhaps by design, had grown increasingly vague about things like that. Such stories, when they appeared, showed up two or three pages in. And on network news, the newscasters mentioned them, but quickly, as if they were reporting on a particularly bad landslide in Peru or Mexico, before moving on to local news, sports, politics, and the weather.

Cora didn't know anyone who had ever visited India or Ethiopia.

They were places, she decided, accustomed to cataclysm and destruction, to cyclones or war or disease or pestilence.

Certainly they had their own facilities. And their own doctors, not as good as American doctors, but capable and, in their ways, heroic. She had read that the medical infrastructure of some Asian countries was almost as good as in the United States, but she didn't really believe it. Bad things happened in places like that, faraway places, crowded places.

Of course, bad things happened here, too. The same bad things that were happening there. Strange to think about all those people on the other side of the world lying down when the sleeps came. All those people with the same problems, the same fear.

She tried not to think about it too much, to wonder what they did with their sleepers.

When people came in the Black Walnut, she evaluated them sometimes, quietly, without even pausing in her work. Would this one wake up, would that one? The Black people would be fine, in whatever world they'd inhabit if a cure was never found. And she looked at them with a kind of curiosity. What must all this mean to that man with the nice shoes and easy laugh? Were the sleeps only a sort of inconvenience for him? Did he know how her stomach tightened up if she thought too much about it? Could he understand, that kind, older Black man with the pleasant laugh who always tipped her well and spoke easily to her, not at all superior, anything but superior. Was pity the source of his kindness, of his tip? Or was he just a kind man? Or both? And should she resent him? Should she be envious? And how did she feel, late at night, having written nothing good at all, having lain awake in bed remembering how she'd seen him in the park, out with his entire family, grilling at the public barbecue laughing, the family so at ease, the boys throwing the football, a toddler with a popsicle dripping redly over her hand. Why shouldn't she resent them just a little bit, there in the middle of the night, alone? It wouldn't be wrong to resent them just a little bit.

+

She walked and walked.

The night before, it had rained in a way that she remembered from her childhood, incessant and soothing, clattering on the roof and windows, the lightning increasingly close and thrilling, at times flashing violently with a simultaneous explosion of thunder. And then the weird silence that followed, a ringing of her bones before the sense of the rain returned, shocking and windswept and wild.

She sat by her bedroom window looking into the night, down to the row of sports bars and the antique mall and the parked cars battered by rain, glittering in the sodium lights. How strange that gray street in the middle of this meaningless little town looked when the lightning flashed over it, illuminating everything yellowly. What a wonderful violence to cleanse the streets and store windows and windshields and sidewalks.

When she woke the next morning, everything was clean and new. She put on her sneakers and walked down West Pine past the train tracks and the grain silos and into the park, down the little trail that edged the water. It was still very early and she was the only one there, standing by the overfull stream bed. The air felt cool and motionless.

A white heron stood among the rocks, very still, its head turning so it could eye her quietly.

"Hello," Cora said.

The heron adjusted its balance on the rocks almost imperceptibly, its focus never leaving her.

"Hello," she said again. "Hello there."

After a very long time, it shifted its footing and looked down quickly, dipping its head into the water, emerging with what looked like a frog. Dangling from the heron's beak, the frog twisted and shuddered and flopped hopelessly.

The heron held it fast, its eyes back on Cora. The frog struggled, then seemed all at once to give up, so it hung limply.

When the heron rose into the air, she could hear the rush of air beneath its great white outstretched wings.

Soon it was out of sight.

Cora waited a moment longer. The stream rushed past and bent to that place where it widened, became more of a river.

There, she saw the beer cans caught among the roots of a tree.

+

Glass lay in bed and fingered the fountain pen Cora had given him. It was beautiful, glimmering bluely in the nightlight, so heavy and firm in his hand. The nib was stamped 14K and Glass let it slide over his cheek so he could feel its intensity.

The pen needed a bottle of ink, but he had none. It didn't matter too much, though. It was beautiful all by itself, and Cora had given it to him.

She had taken it out of her purse and said, "Here, you keep it," and when he took it, she smiled at him and said, "Friends?"

"Friends," he'd said.

And she nodded. He would never have told on her and he felt a little ashamed at having even brought it up. The pen caught the light and glittered meanly.

The house was silent. The wasps were in the dark garage crawling the passages from aquarium to aquarium.

Glass thought about the house he grew up in, all closed up and dark. His father's night table and all the contents therein, the wristwatch and the old IDs and the keys. His own bedroom and his many collections, his bottlecaps and coins and projectile points and meteorites. He wanted to go there forever, to live there all by himself, but he couldn't figure out how. It didn't seem possible. It was a stupid fantasy.

He lay in bed and held the fountain pen above his head, turning it over and over until he fell asleep.

+

Because there had been some warning—sleeps of great intensity had followed the weather up from Oklahoma and Arkansas—people were grave and serious all day after the storms passed. The Black Walnut Pub closed up early, and when Cora walked past the BI-LO, she saw people pushing shopping carts overloaded with paper towels and toilet paper and canned goods. What would they do with toilet paper if they fell asleep and never woke up, she wondered. What was the purpose of canned goods if a tube was going to feed you? But there they were, loading the beds of pickup trucks with canned beans and tinned ham, with paper towels and beer.

They lined up at the Sunoco, filling their cars with gas, filling their red plastic gas cans until the pumps ran dry.

Fuck it, she thought, and kept walking up Maguire Street past the Walgreens and Famous Rick's BBQ and to that part of the old town where the red brick buildings were, the courthouse and the library and the bars and the cute bed-and-breakfast, its living room filled with Victoriana, with German porcelain dolls and lamps with stained glass shades, and the old man and his friend who ran it—everyone knew they were gay, but everyone liked them too, so they didn't talk about it that much.

She was standing in front of the statue of Daniel Boone, looking up at his enormous, rigid metal face when she heard the siren singing from the edges of town.

She swallowed a tablet of Eight and stood by the side of the road looking up toward the university.

She felt the first wave of sleep hit after about five minutes and it penetrated the Eight almost completely, so she wobbled and grabbed at a signpost for balance. She could see not stars, but the force of blackness closing in at the corners of her eyes, then more, so she felt as though she were observing the spinning barber pole across Maguire Street through a cardboard mailing tube, then through a drinking straw, and finally a sort of white explosion in her head as the Eight kicked in at last.

Stars, stars, stars.

She was awake. And the city was asleep.

+

For more than two minutes she felt multitudinous. She stood by the looming statue, its shotgun balanced on its shoulder. And she lay on the grass farther up the courthouse lawn. She leaned against the brick wall of Hero's Bar & Grille. She did these things simultaneously, as if three photographic slides had been stacked on top of one another and held to the light, each taken at different times, from different angles. Over time the angles had widened, the time between them stretched. Sometimes the Eight threw her back in time an hour. Once, it seemed to throw her forward in time. But today she stayed near the courthouse lawn, multitudinous.

As her brain absorbed the Eight, her sense of time returned, the knowledge that she had, in fact, walked from the statue across the lawn and down the block.

She sat for another minute on the curb and held her head to her knees as the predictable headache washed over her, smothered her, blinded her, then retreated to the back of her head, where it would go on throbbing for a while.

Up the road, a car horn blared and blared. Someone must have fallen asleep in the driver's seat, head against the horn.

When her vision finally cleared, she stood. The street was empty. It was about noon and the bars and stores were locked and empty. Through the Town Tavern window, she could see the television playing to no one, a sitcom and then a commercial for toothpaste, a woman smiling, her teeth gleaming weirdly.

She didn't know what to do. She'd parked Jake's Datsun behind the courthouse, and she walked there, through the silence. The sky clouded up, but it didn't look like rain. Just the grayness of fall, and she climbed into the car and drove past the churches and the high school. All was quiet. Now and then she saw someone who had been caught by surprise, asleep on a front lawn or in a parked car. One little boy lay half in the road and half on the sidewalk, his bicycle on its side by a couple of garbage cans, as if he had been hurrying home too late, too late.

Cora stopped, got out, and dragged his sleeping body out of the road.

The BI-LO parking lot was nearly full, and when she walked up to the doors, they slid open easily. An instrumental version of a Beach Boys song was playing. The store was vast and silent.

Shoppers slept in the aisles, their carts filled with whatever was still available when the sirens rang—tinned sardines, pickles, paper napkins. Cora walked among them. Their purses splayed out on the floor, shoppers asleep in pools of milk, among dropped green peppers. What was her name? Rhonda Sampson? She saw Rhonda Sampson, who taught medieval literature at the university, asleep in the candy aisle, a bag of Twizzlers by her side.

Now it was the Beatles's "Love Me Do," playing, but instrumental again. Orchestral. She walked back by the meat counter, where a young man had fallen asleep holding a baby, who was also asleep, both of them lying on the linoleum floor. The baby had a bad cut on its cheek and Cora dabbed at it with a paper napkin. The father had dropped a jar of Ragú spaghetti sauce as they fell and it stained the floor garishly, like blood in a horror movie.

In the back of the store, where only employees were allowed, she found two crates of rice. These she loaded in a shopping cart and wheeled through the store to her car. She couldn't have explained to herself why, except that it made her feel secure to have all that rice.

She found a case of canned soup in the back, too. And black beans.

+

At the far end of the store, in the wine and beer aisle, she ran into a young woman, her eyes wide and strange. She reminded Cora for a moment of her sister, her sister grown wan. She had curly blond hair and she wore jeans that were too tight and a red, overlarge T-shirt that floated around her hips. Cora thought she recognized her from some bar or other, but had never spoken to her. She was loading a cart with bottles of white wine.

"Hey," Cora said, holding onto her shopping cart. The woman looked up at her, startled. "It's all right," Cora said. "You got Eight, right?"

The woman nodded, then smiled. "Yeah," she said. "Yeah." She put a couple more bottles in her cart, then brushed her hair out of her eyes. She had a tattoo of an eye on the back of her thick hand.

"I knew there must be at least a few of us, right?"

The woman nodded. "More than a few. But not too many. You scared me."

Cora tried to smile. "Sorry."

"It's cool," she said. "Look, I don't mean to be rude, but I gotta get out of here before everyone wakes up. My boyfriend's waiting for me in the car."

They looked at each other. The fluorescent lights buzzed above them.

“Do you know where I can get more?” Cora asked her.

“More what?”

“More Eight.”

The woman laughed a low, quick contemptuous laugh.

“I’m down to just a handful,” Cora said.

“Hold on to them,” the woman said, loading another bottle into her overfull cart. “You’ll never see another one.”

And then she pushed her cart down the aisle, past the sleepers, past the registers. The doors slid open for her.

Hawaiian music now, descending like warm rain from the speakers that hung among the ceiling tiles.

+

Cora watched as the woman loaded those bottles into the back seat of a beat-up old Volkswagen bug. A young man had come out from the driver’s seat to help her, a lean blond young man wearing a honey-colored jacket with a lot of fringe, a jacket that was really too big for him. At first Cora took him for a boy, he was so slight and quick, but then she could see that he was not a boy at all. It was hard to tell how old he was.

When the woman pointed at Cora, who was standing by the sliding doors, Cora smiled and waved. The man considered her, then smiled and waved back. He had too many white teeth.

Had she seen him somewhere before?

“You better get some free drinks while they’re still asleep,” he called, as the woman loaded the last of the bottles into the trunk.

And Cora smiled. “OK,” she called back.

“Cheers!” He smiled and climbed back into the car. And then they were gone.

+

How she had loved literature. How simple that love had been. When a high school teacher had told her to memorize a poem, she had picked the longest and hardest in the textbook, "The Love Song of J. Alfred Prufrock." She read it over and over again, memorizing stanza by stanza until that strange poem's rhythms sunk deep under her skin and she could feel them moving around inside her, in her veins and lungs and gut.

The yellow smoke that filled the poem filled her mind, strange and cinematic, billowing down bygone London streets, lit by lamplight, dangerous and lonely and acrid. The movements of the mind within the poem startled her. She hadn't yet learned that a living mind might conceal itself beneath the surfaces of any poem or novel or play, that great writing might enact, might *become*, the currents and tides of a mind struggling against an unsolvable problem, a problem that consumed it, that it examined and considered and felt, ending so beautifully in ambiguity or complexity or loss.

Had anyone asked her then what "The Love Song" actually meant, she wouldn't have been able to say. But, unlike her friends, she held onto the poem's truths and she walked around the house reciting lines in her head, "I grow old, I grow old, I shall wear the bottoms of my trousers rolled. I grow old, old, I shall wear them rolled, I shall wear them. Rolled."

The lines sang inside her as she did the dishes or emptied the garbage or watched TV.

How driven she had been in college to learn the language of literature, to understand the slippery Romantic poets, the Russian novelists, their yearnings for purity and simplicity and perfection among London's and Moscow's smokestacks and distractions. And the plays of Shaw and Shakespeare, and Genet, the characters whose motivations and yearnings and objectives were often obscure even to them, but fascinating to Cora, who found she had a gift for writing dialogue and so composed scene after scene in her mind while her roommates drank beer or skipped classes or talked for hours on the phone with boyfriends back home in Kearney.

Later she had learned to dissect a play, and having dissected it perfectly, having earned an A+ in literary dissection, she found the work no longer moved her as it once had, when she could not have explained it entirely or articulated quite how it moved.

She began writing her own stories and plays, late at night with her notebook and cigarettes, writing and rewriting, moving scenes around and asking herself, Just what is this character thinking? Whose thoughts are these? And whose words?, realizing for the first time that they were both hers and not hers.

She had won the student fiction prize and the drama prize and a fellowship to study dramatic writing in Iowa, where she got to hear other playwrights pick apart her plays and put them back together again while she sat in a windowless classroom silently taking notes, then returned to her little duplex to rewrite, rewrite, rewrite.

Now, a few years later, here she was and the mystery of drama and story seemed to have worn away, to have revealed something far less interesting beneath its skin: gears and cogs, rules of composition to be conveyed to bored students, networks of symbols to be explained or recreated. What had startled and confounded her in college became, in her late twenties, artifacts that she could understand and explain, a series of models she could build with grace and skill and as easily deconstruct.

That was why, when she lost her teaching position at the university, she didn't look for another one, but stayed in town and took another job, any job. She hadn't stayed for Jake or any other man. She stayed because she wanted to do something, anything, but dissect literature, hoping somehow to rediscover that sense of wonder she'd once had.

For some reason, a line of Eliot crossed her mind as she drove away from the BI-LO, twenty pounds of rice and beans, soup, and a few bottles of wine in the trunk. “Do I dare to eat a peach? Do I dare to eat a peach?” That boy was still asleep in the grass by his bicycle. As she drove past, her eyes fixed on a long gash across his cheek. She hadn’t noticed that before.

Her problems were meaningless and omnipresent. Literature was meaningless dust. She would never rediscover it, she thought. She read trashy horror novels now.

The town had been asleep for nearly an hour. Too long, too long.

+

The children had been sent home from school. The sleep storm would be too big—that’s what they called it sometimes, a *sleep storm*, like it was only another kind of weather. So Taft Junior High opened its doors at 10:30 and Glass and everyone else spilled onto the chilly playground. It didn’t matter that he’d barely done his homework, that he’d filled in the math assignment with nearly random numbers, that he’d only skimmed the short story in his language arts textbook. No one would be the wiser today and he was free, and he and Scooby stood on the playground. “Later this afternoon?” Glass said and Scooby nodded, said, “Sure, yeah, later,” and they parted ways.

He dawdled on his way home, kicking a pine cone down the middle of the street, rattling a stick between the metal spokes of a wrought iron fence. The sleeps had become routine to him, nothing really to worry about, just something that once had seemed strange but was strange no longer.

Shane was already home, having picked up Carlos at his school, and Carlos was going on about Japanese throwing stars and Bruce Lee.

“Uh-huh,” Shane said, looking at his watch, then locking the doors, front and back. He seemed distracted and when Glass said he might take his bicycle out for a bit, Shane told him he couldn't, no, sorry, not until after he woke up.

"But they haven't even blown the siren!" Glass said. "I mean, I'll have ten minutes once they blow the siren. At least."

Shane shook his head, seeming drawn and strange, because he'd heard from more than a few people that this was going to be a long one, a bad one, they were saying it was really bad down in Springfield, a lot of people not waking up, so he suggested a card game instead. "How about a game of spades?"

But Carlos didn't want to play spades and neither did Glass, and finally they settled on Sorry!, which they played twice, the TV talking in the background, cartoons and puppets and a show about an old lady detective.

When Shane laughed, Glass could tell it was forced, that he was trying to make things seem normal, and when they finally heard the sirens wailing from the edges of town, it was almost a relief to climb into their twin beds, to see Shane lie down on the mat between them and close his eyes.

And when Glass woke fifty-six minutes later, he had the whole afternoon in front of him and his first thought was to walk over to Scooby's house and tell him about the strange dream he had had, the dream about watching that same play—always an outdoor theater, always the same play. But now the boy and the woman had made a home of the brightly painted minibus, and the surroundings had changed, as if they'd driven the minibus to a new location, a ruined gas station by the side of the highway. And they seemed happy, the two of them in lawn chairs beside the van, talking about old times, the times before the world changed, and as they talked, a young man was sidling their way, was walking with a sort of wobble.

And still, atop the minibus, that black angel, crouched, half visible, its wings curled tight around it.

And always in the audience beside him, that sense of his father.

And I was there, too, sitting a few rows back, only half paying attention to the play.

+

Glass lay in bed, awake, trying to recollect the details of his dream. He heard Carlos shift and then sit up.

Glass said, "I had such a crazy dream this time. A guy with wings was crouching on top of a minibus, and that woman and boy were at a gas station, but I don't know where, and there was another man just watching me and taking notes," but Carlos wasn't looking at him or really listening. He was looking at Shane, who was lying on his back on the mat, fast asleep, his blanket bunched up around his shoulders. Shane shifted, turned over, and sighed heavily, but he did not wake up.

"Dad?" said Carlos.

5 EIGHT TRACK

Much later you might come across a house with an X chalked on the door. That meant there was a sleeper in the house, a sleeper who needed to be taken away, to be processed. But that was in the future, after the story I'm telling you ends.

For now you simply called a toll-free number and waited on hold for a while, and when at last someone answered, you gave your address and confirmed that the patient was not wakeable. This, Glass was able to do.

The green-and-yellow vans arrived in town from Jefferson City to the east and from Kansas City to the west. They arrived from Maryville and Springfield. After the big sleep, the vans drove up and down the streets, and polite men and women with their notepads and addresses loaded the sleepers onto the folding bunks. Papers were signed and carbon copies left behind with telephone numbers and facility numbers and then the vans eased away. Each van held six sleepers and could transport twelve sleepers a day to the facility two hours south of town. The facility to the west was already full, or so people heard.

When the van pulled up at Carlos's house, the young woman who helped load Shane onto the sixth and final bunk asked the boys if they had an adult caretaker.

"Yes," said Carlos quietly.

"And who is that?" she asked, holding her clipboard.

"My mother," Carlos said.

Glass shifted on the big easy chair. He was looking out the window at the bird feeder. A large red bird seemed to look back at him for a moment, then it went back to the birdseed. Glass sipped his Coke.

"And where is your mother?" The woman was trying to sound sympathetic, but it came out all wrong, like she'd been doing it all day. "Is she in town?" she said, speaking very slowly and too loudly, like she was talking to a very old woman, someone who couldn't understand.

"She's in Cleveland," Carlos said softly. He wouldn't look at her. He looked at his dirty tennis shoes. Then he gave her the address.

"Cleveland's pretty far away," the woman said. "Do you have anyone here in town?"

Carlos shook his head.

"No one at all?" she said. She was writing on her clipboard.

"I don't know," Carlos said. "I mean, who?"

Glass sipped his Coke. He didn't like the woman that much, but she had a job to do.

"Can I have your mother's phone number in Cleveland?" the woman asked, and Carlos gave it to her. "Thank you," she said.

Then she looked at Glass. "And you are . . . ?" she said.

The red bird was looking at him again through the glass. "I'm Charles," Glass said. "I've been living here, that's all. I'm a friend."

A swarthy man came in from outside, the guy who drove the van. He raised his eyebrows as if to say *hurry up*. She looked back at him and shook her head quickly, as if to say *not yet*.

"Charles," she said, "do you have someone local who can look after you?"

"I can look after myself pretty well," he said. "I mean, until things get back to normal."

The woman pursed her lips. "No adult at all?" she said. She clearly needed to write something down on her form.

"I don't know." He felt the long silence.

The driver lingered in the doorway. The woman coughed.

"Well," he said at last, "yes."

"There's an adult who can . . . look after you?"

"Yes," Glass said more firmly. "Cora Gardner. She's my aunt," he said.

Carlos looked at him, confused, but he didn't say anything.

"Do you have her address and telephone number?"

Of course, he knew Cora's address. He'd walked past her building dozens of times, there between the Town Tavern and Java Junction, just above the Hero's Bar & Grille. "I have her address," he said, and he gave it to her. "I don't have her telephone number. I usually just go over there."

"And will you be going over there now?"

"Yes," Glass lied.

+

Shane's house felt very strange without Shane in it—quiet and foreign and small. Glass made Carlos a sandwich and one for himself but Carlos wouldn't eat. And he wouldn't talk, either.

"You OK?" Glass asked him, but he knew that wasn't the right question.

"I'm OK," said Carlos, who wasn't. He just looked at his sandwich, then, after a while, walked into the garage to tend to his wasps. When Glass looked in on him an hour later, Carlos was staring into the lunar aquarium unblinking, watching a little black wasp traverse an enormous crater. "I'm OK," said Carlos.

Glass thought about calling Scooby. Maybe they could sleep over there. But he didn't. The caretaker the woman in the van had promised to send didn't show up that evening, and Glass watched

TV. The newscasters were talking about a cure. The young blond anchor smiled at the camera, and then there was footage of a lab, men in white coats with test tubes, and then the anchor again. Progress had been made, progress was being made, and then a commercial for back pills, always that commercial running over and over again. "Oh, my aching back!" said the housewife.

And then the phone rang. It was Carlos's mother. She had just heard, and Carlos pulled the phone cord as taut as he could so he could talk in the hallway, where Glass couldn't hear. But Glass could hear. Carlos said *yes*, and *yes*, and yes he wanted to and yes he could be ready by tomorrow, and then after a while he hung up.

When Glass looked in on him, he was packing his suitcase.

"I'm going to Cleveland," he said.

"You can't go to Cleveland," Glass told him.

"Why not?"

"Because how are you going to get there?"

"There's the train," Carlos said. "It stops in Chicago and goes on to Cleveland. My mother bought me a ticket. I can pick it up at the station."

"Oh," said Glass. He felt a little dizzy.

"What will you do?" Carlos asked him.

"I dunno," said Glass. "I mean, I dunno. I'll get by."

"Who's Cora Gardner?" Carlos said. "She's not your aunt or you'd have been living with her all this time."

"Just a friend."

"Will you look after my wasps?"

+

The train station was only a fifteen-minute walk away, though it took longer the next morning because they had to drag Carlos's two suitcases. They were so heavy that both boys pushed hard to get them up the little steps onto the train, and even then the porter had to help them.

When Glass got back to Shane's house, he took the tops off the various aquariums to let the wasps out. They rose into the air and hummed around the garage until he found the garage door opener. He would leave the door open for a while, so they could escape. They hummed out into the late morning air.

But that evening, when Glass went into the garage to check on the aquariums, all the wasps were back, crawling dumbly over the blinking Christmas tree and across the tiny windmills. He stood there for a few minutes watching them feed on the little sponge soaked with wasp nectar. He dropped a few bits of peach into one of the aquariums.

They would never leave.

Glass never saw Carlos again.

+

After she'd stolen the rice and beans and soup and wine, Cora thought she had enough time to fill the car with gas. But there were lines of people asleep in their cars at the gas pumps, long silent lines, the drivers slumped over, heads on their steering wheels. An old Asian woman lay fast asleep on the asphalt in front of one of the pumps. Also a fat man, his wallet on the ground behind him.

One by one, she pushed the slumped-over drivers aside and eased their cars forward into various parking spots. She dragged the Asian woman as gently as she could onto the grass by the road, but she couldn't move the fat man.

When she created just enough room to pull Jake's Datsun in, she filled the tank.

It was a beautiful day and she felt like the only living thing on earth. The gas pump ticked and ticked, one gallon after another.

From everywhere, she heard car horns blaring, blaring, and could imagine the drivers asleep, their foreheads pressing the horns.

Once the tank was filled, she walked into the gas station and, in a storeroom in the back, found five or six red plastic gas cans. She filled these, too, and stowed them in the back of the car with the food. That made her feel safer, too.

At the time, she couldn't have explained why she did this. Just a few hours earlier, she'd scoffed at the people lined up at the gas stations, the people pushing shopping carts full of tinned ham to their cars, but something had changed in her. The duration of the sleep, the strength of it working against the Eight in her system. The force of that sleep had nearly penetrated the Eight.

When she'd filled the gas cans and pulled away from the gas station, she saw the first stirring of life among the sleeping, a young man lifting his head from the steering wheel of his parked car and rubbing his eyes.

She was going to need more Eight. Who did Jake work for? Jimbo, he'd told her that evening long ago. Jim-Bo. Jimbo might still have Eight, not that she could afford to buy any. Or that girl and her boyfriend at the BI-LO. They must have had a few tabs, whoever they were. Jimbo was the more promising source.

She'd already asked Jake's friends about him and they didn't know. They'd told her it was best just to roll with the sleeps, just roll with them until there was a cure.

Always, she remembered that moment when the back of her head smacked the diving board, that instantaneous certainty that blackness would come, that she could not control it just before it did come, just before it snuffed her out.

+

This was why Cora searched through the glove compartment of Jake's Datsun, never finding any scrap of paper or address that might lead her to anyone named Jimbo. And this was why she asked all his friends again if they'd heard of such a person. And it was why she found herself lurking outside Jake's sister's house one chilly afternoon in late October. The little blue pickup truck hadn't left the driveway in two hours, and Cora had walked around and around the block, pretending to listen to her Walkman, though the batteries had died. Alone with her thoughts, all alone, thinking of her sister in Omaha, who wouldn't speak to her, who wouldn't answer her calls, her sister's husband, how she had wanted to touch his arm, his chest, and then turning the corner she saw that the pickup was at last gone.

Cora had been in the house before and she quickly slipped around to the back door. She tried two or three keys from his key ring before she found the right one, unlocked the door, and walked inside.

The carpet was yellow shag. An open can of Tab and a tumbler full of melting ice sat on the coffee table. A cat slept in a square of sunlight on an old upright piano. There were six cats, Cora remembered. Cora patted the cat, looked around the quiet living room, then walked toward what she remembered was Jake's room, though she'd only been in it once, when his sister was out of town and he'd wanted to find a particular cassette tape to play for her. The whole house smelled of cigarettes.

The room was mostly cleared out now. A twin bed, stripped, and a turntable on a low shelf in the corner. A dresser. Several boxes in the closet. Everything that made the room Jake's had been cleared away: the lava lamp, the stolen Howard Johnson porcelain ashtrays, the boots and jean jackets and Guatemalan woven knapsack and rows of LPs and books on magick and spies and altered worlds—everything, everything was gone, was scrubbed away. The carpet had been vacuumed. Cora could see the thick stripes the vacuum cleaner had made in it.

She knelt on the floor, looking into the closet, looking at the boxes. In the first box she found only records. The second one too—nothing but records. In the third were framed photographs, a scrapbook, a story Jake had written and illustrated as a child, about a penguin who floated away on an iceberg all the way to Chicago. Cora read some of it before placing it to the side.

What had happened to Jake's clothing? Had his sister simply sold it? Or donated it? How could Jake, whom she never loved, whom she had certainly liked, how could Jake be reduced to five boxes? The room had been such a wonderful mess last year.

And what had happened to his address book? Did he have a datebook? She couldn't remember. Probably not. What dates did Jake have to remember?

There was a shoebox, up on the closet's top shelf, but she couldn't reach it. The house was silent. Two cats had drifted into the room. One was asleep on the bed and the other observed her from the door with bright green, unblinking eyes.

She was thinking about going to the kitchen to get a chair when she heard the back door open and close. Then a rustling of bags and the sound of car keys on the counter.

The cats slipped from Jake's bedroom toward the sound and then Cora heard Jake's sister's voice: "Good kitty," she was saying, "good, good, good. Now Pluto, that's not for you. That's for Henrietta," and then the sound of dry cat food tinkling into cat dishes, one for each of the six cats. Cora hid herself in the closet and closed the door, though she'd left Jake's bedroom a mess, his boxes all over the floor, half emptied.

+

After a day at Shane's house, Glass dragged his suitcase back to his old house.

He missed his own room, the bright yellow floral wallpaper and forest-green carpeting, the collections of shells and plumbing equipment and agates that he kept in his many boxes. He missed his father's room, the little puck-shaped can of Copenhagen snuff. He held it to his nose until his father's complete image appeared before him and he held it in his mind's eye until, a moment later, it wavered and disappeared.

He ran his finger across his father's collection of books, hundreds of books on archaeology and military history and Word War II and Custer and the election of 1876 and the Gunpowder Plot and on and on it went. On the spines of the books he'd read, his father had placed a circular red sticker so he wouldn't accidentally read them again.

There were no novels among his father's books. The only poetry was by Archibald MacLeish or Erich Kästner.

Glass walked slowly around the house. Here was the row of stone tools and African fetishes and grinding stones and great Indian pots on the shelves in the brightly lit study. He looked at pictures of naked dark men unembarrassed and smiling for invisible cameramen, holding up spears or odd feathered objects, and Glass smiled at them. He fingered the ribbons and small medals of European wars his father kept hidden away in an antique linen chest.

The refrigerator was empty, and Glass stared into its glowing whiteness for a while before closing the door.

That afternoon it rained hard, and Glass lay on his father's bed looking up at the ceiling. The wallpaper was blue and floral and he stared at it until the flowers blurred and became a blue haze that hovered above him. It wouldn't stop raining and Glass was getting hungry. He would have to buy something to eat, but where was his father's wallet?

It was in his briefcase in the closet by his boots and there was money in it and an ATM card. Glass knew the PIN. It was his own birthday: 1022. But it was raining wildly now, far too hard to go out, so he stayed inside listening to the rain on the rooftop and watching through the windows as it pooled on the sidewalk, as it filled the street.

Would the basement fill with water? This had happened a few times before and his father had drained it with sump pumps and hoses, which he'd stretched down the driveway. Now, Glass walked down into it, moving half-soaked boxes off the floor and onto any dry surface he could find: the washing machine, an old desk, a battered love seat. The water rose and it rained into the evening and the trees swayed blackly in the wet wind, lit by lightning.

On their shelves the Indian skulls grinned at him. So many skulls in the quiet basement, so many boxes of bones catalogued and cross-referenced, his father's work half done and strange to Glass, who knew only the age of things and nothing more.

When he'd moved the boxes and the abandoned laundry, Glass stood shoeless in the ankle-deep water for a while, holding one of those skulls in his hands, turning it over and over. It had once been a real person. He looked into its eyeholes and felt the weight of the cranium.

And then he was crying. He couldn't stop. He didn't even try to stop. He didn't know what to do or where to go or how to stop crying. He didn't know how to get the water out of the basement or how to drive a car or how to get groceries home from the supermarket or what to do about Carlos's wasps.

+

Scooby's family was perfect. It was a perfect family, Glass thought. Scooby had brothers and a little sister and a mother and a father. They were kind to Glass and gave him cookies after school if he came by to watch TV or play Atari. Scooby shared a room with one brother, and the other three boys lived in the refinished basement and his little sister had her own tiny room, and Mrs. Franklin was beautiful. Mrs. Franklin had a deep rich laugh, Glass thought, so different from his father's friends at the university who chuckled wryly over some insinuation or other that Glass couldn't understand.

And the Franklins were safe, they were safe, they would not fall asleep forever, even if no one ever found a cure. Probably not, anyway. Scooby's father was large and round and led the Cub Scout pack when the Cub Scouts met, which hadn't been recently. He smoked little black cigarettes in the backyard and he smelled sweet and sharp, like tobacco. Sometimes he played horseshoes with Scooby and Glass in the backyard. He was awful at horseshoes and Scooby, victorious, would dance around and wave his arms.

Glass thought about the Franklins as he stood ankle deep in water holding that Indian skull, crying. He wanted to be in that family, safe from all this and normal. He wanted his life to be normal again.

But he couldn't go to them. He would be an imposition, a doomed boy among their kindnesses. He didn't want that.

+

"I wasn't," Cora said.

"Yes, you was," said Karen, Jake's sister.

"What was I stealing then?" said Cora. She was standing among the open boxes. "What?"

"You was stealing LPs, I'll bet. And other valuables. You probably stole his car, too."

Cora had parked the car around the corner and now she was glad, at least, of that. She looked around on the floor. "There's nothing valuable here," she said at last. "Besides, you know me. I'm Jake's friend."

Cora had hoped to hide quietly in the closet until nightfall, then sneak out, but she'd been in there less than an hour when Karen opened the door to Jake's room, turned on the light, and saw the mess of boxes.

"If you wasn't stealing, then what?"

"I was looking for something of mine," Cora said. "Something I lent him. He was going to give it back before he fell asleep."

Karen looked at her quietly for a moment. "What thing?" she asked.

But Cora couldn't think of anything. A yellow cat walked into the room, then out again. "Something personal," she said at last.

"No," Karen said. "You was stealing."

"No, really, I think it's in that shoebox on the top shelf," said Cora.

Karen looked at the red-and-blue shoebox, then back at Cora. "That's what you lent him? In the shoebox?"

"Yes," said Cora. "I think that might be it."

"You lent him a box of his own baby pictures?"

And then she was walking toward the telephone and Cora pushed right on past her, ran through the living room, out the door, and into the street, having found nothing at all, having made a fool of herself again.

+

This was why she arrived at work late and got a lecture from Wanda, who said it had to stop, the lateness, the clumsiness, though Tina could easily have handled the early-evening tables, probably would have appreciated the extra tips. Still, Cora apologized, said it wouldn't happen again, no, never again, and Wanda nodded. "Don't let it," she said, and Cora worked until close, until that last blond kid in his leather fringe jacket, until that last plump girl with leg warmers and a university T-shirt, until all the laggers and sippers left. Then she stacked the chairs on the tables and swept and sponged the counters while Tina busied herself in the kitchen cleaning the griddle, washing the beer glasses.

Every now and then someone would walk past on the street outside. She wanted to be there, outside in the cool night air, and when they were finally finished and she walked out onto the sidewalk, a kind of relief swept over her. She told herself Karen probably hadn't called the police, not over something so stupid. All day, she'd just felt so apologetic—about everything. About stealing from Jake and hiding in his closet. About screwing up at work. About her sister. Her sister had been weighing on her more than anything in her life, and she repented of that horrible stupid evening, her sister's stupid handsome husband—she couldn't bring herself to even think his name—in her stupid arms.

She couldn't blame it on him, either, not really. She had been charmed by his flirtations. She had been flattered. And she envied her sister. All their lives, Cora had been good at things. Cora had won prizes. Great things were in store for Cora, everyone said. But, in truth, people *liked* Susan more. Susan was kind and fun and lively and plump. When she smiled, her smile was genuine and her cheeks grew flushed, her voice conspiratorial and inviting, and it didn't matter that she got Bs and Cs in school and didn't play any sports, because she hardly cared about that kind of thing. She cared about you, she wanted to know what you thought, how you felt, and people liked that, too.

So, maybe there had been some malice in Cora when she kissed that man, her sister's man, when she let him touch her and unbutton her blouse. Maybe she had not discouraged his flirtations all summer because for once she felt not just admired but wanted. He wanted her, or seemed to.

And then the incident with the horse barn and Cora so blind drunk she wasn't even sure what was happening, while her sister's husband hosed the place down and she groped her way to her bedroom only to wake the next morning with that horrible creeping feeling that something had gone very wrong, but what was it? She couldn't remember, and then suddenly she did remember and she got out of bed and looked out the window. The side of the horse barn was blackened with soot and char, and "You'd better go," her sister had told her after she had dressed and made her way to the kitchen, stupid and hungover. "We both think you'd better go."

That had been right before the Sinaloan condition had hit the newspapers, right before those people in Sinaloa fell asleep for thirty seconds, over a hundred thousand people all at once and the whole world was amazed.

Cora had moved to Missouri, had taken a job teaching writing to sophomores.

Her sister would hardly speak to her, her sister who was really her only family in the world. Her cousins hardly counted and she'd only met her father once in her memory—he'd come by "to get to know his girls," and she and Susan both had said they didn't want to know him, thank you, no, they were just fine as they were. She'd felt apologetic about that afterward, too.

Now she had no one. And for that she was truly sorry. She wanted to tell her sister, but when she called her, her sister's voice was cold. "You know," Susan told her, "you got everything. All the talent, all the brains, all the attention. I had one thing. I had Richard, and you know what? You know what?"

"I'm sorry," Cora had said.

"You had to make that . . . impure."

"I didn't mean—"

"Yes, I think you did," Susan told her, before hanging up.

+

Tonight Cora was trying to feel good, to push those thoughts away. She was done with work. She had a bad day behind her. She walked from the Black Walnut down Maguire Street and felt the cold fill her windbreaker and ruffle her hair. The courthouse loomed, grotesque, Victorian and spooky in the night air. And the statue of

Daniel Boone, lit from below, was ghastly and imposing and silly. A few lines from "Prufrock" crossed her mind:

> The yellow fog that rubs its back upon the windowpanes,
> The yellow smoke that rubs its muzzle on the windowpanes,
> Licked its tongue into the corners of the evening.

It was such an evening, a low fog rolling in, lit by streetlamps. The smell of cold rain in the air.

She should write tonight. She had had an idea for a play, and she should write it. It would be a play about running away from problems, about getting into a minibus and just driving, driving—and the adventures of leaving a hard life, and the fact that the hard life would always follow one, would always follow. Why hadn't she written in so long? Because she was tired from waiting tables? Because she had no one really to talk to? Because of the sleeps? She didn't know, but she meant to write tonight, to pour herself a big glass of red wine and write a play about a family and a minibus and an escape.

When she turned the corner onto West Pine, she could see that the bars were still lit and she could hear the music throbbing from them. No police car was parked in front of her building. She thought about maybe a few drinks at the Town Tavern, a game of pool, she would change into her jeans and a T-shirt, but no. She would write. She would write.

But when she neared her apartment she saw someone sitting on her front steps, someone hunched over and reading a book in the light that shone through the bar windows.

This person wore a dark windbreaker with the hood up over his head. He turned the page of his book and then, sensing her presence, looked right up at her. After a moment she recognized him. It was that boy from the river, the one from the Office Supply & Typewriter Repair, the one she'd given the pen to, the boy with the scars on his face. She couldn't remember his name.

"I just need a place to stay," he said.

6 THE GUN

She told him he could stay a few days if he promised to go to school and do all the things a kid his age was supposed to do, and he said he would. And he did, walking down the apartment steps every morning at 8:00 and returning from school at 3:30, then riding off on his bicycle again to find Scooby or a couple other friends.

"If I hear about you skipping school," she told him several times during those first weeks, "you can't stay here anymore. You've got to go to school."

And, Jesus, she thought, his story was the worst one she'd come across—lost his mother to Minnesota somehow, lost his father to the sleeps, lost his foster father the same way. He was all alone, he was more alone than she was. Once or twice she thought about calling Child Protective Services, or whatever they were called, then felt ashamed of herself for considering it.

And now here he was, two months later, sitting on her sofa reading a book about this computer that takes over the world, a book he seemed to have read several times, because the pages were worn and ripped in places. He hummed and turned the page, his mouth moving a little as he read. At night she could hear him crying sometimes and didn't know what to do. Didn't know whether to come into the living room where he slept on the sofa, or just let him cry himself to sleep. When once she came out, he blushed and said he was sorry, he wasn't crying, he must have been dreaming is all. So when he cried she let him cry. And when he read his book, she moved around silently or she asked him about it.

He told her about the book in detail and she nodded and pretended to be very interested and even asked questions about Amanda. How did she know the men in brown suits were agents of Microvac? How did she know that the trick to escaping them wasn't running away, but blending in with the other children, the children who were victims of mind control?

And how did she blend in? Did she just wander around looking glassy eyed?

And Glass would explain with patient detail. He told her he had read the first six volumes of *The Microvac Chronicles* and was waiting for the seventh, which would be published soon, and he would be the first get it because volume six had ended in a particularly dire situation, though they all ended in dire situations, of course. Where he was now, at the end of the fifth volume, Amanda, with the aid of two comrades, had finally found the Central Processor, the main computer that controlled all the cable boxes in all the houses in America, and thus controlled the minds of millions of Americans. She had found it and was on the point of disabling it—she had the codes and needed only to type them into the keyboard in the vast Processing Chamber, empty now because of the power shutdown Amanda had caused to happen—when one of her two comrades smiled wickedly and laughed. He had betrayed her. He had betrayed the Resistance and tricked Amanda. The keyboard wasn't connected to the mainframe at all, it never was. Even now the Guardians of Microvac were on their way with their mind-control devices.

+

They had driven to his father's house a few times now to get his things. Then Cora and a couple friends had hauled the kid's dresser and bookshelf to her apartment, too, so now her living room, which had once been sparsely furnished, was crowded with furniture. The kid slept on the couch, dutifully putting his pillow and blankets away in the closet each morning.

These days, business was up at the Black Walnut, the customers unusually boisterous, often arriving in the evenings a little bit drunk and leaving quite a lot drunker, forgetting their umbrellas under the tables, their wallets and reading glasses and checkbooks. So the evening shift grew hard, but lucrative, guests tending to overtip in their jollity and making a larger mess of the place. For many evenings in a row, she wouldn't see Glass at all, arriving after he'd gone to bed, then sleeping in while he got himself off to school.

She'd grown fond of him, sometimes standing over the sofa as he lay under his green-and-blue *E.T.* blanket, knees pulled up to his chest, fast asleep in her dark living room, her eyes on the long pink scar on his cheek, nothing but the sound of the refrigerator ticking and humming, a distant car horn heard through an open window, the occasional fizz of the sodium lights over West Pine Street. Sometimes he seemed to her to glow in the dark, and she wanted to reach down and run her finger over his scar, to feel it or erase it.

Was it because of her dread that her mind kept returning to Susan?

For a few weeks, knowing Glass was asleep on the sofa or at school or out with Scooby, she thought about her sister less. She didn't lie awake at night going over that stupid evening two years ago, the drunken, reeling dread when she realized the stable was on fire, how she staggered about the yard calling for help because she couldn't even see in front of her, couldn't find the hose, couldn't place one foot in front of the other. If those thoughts encroached on her, she had only to imagine Glass as he was, asleep in the next room, curled on the sofa, one arm under his head, his brown hair rumpled, and she felt better. She felt less a fool. Less a failure.

+

As fall turned to winter and then to spring, attendance got light at school. Mrs. Kogan failed to show up one day in November. Had she fallen asleep, Glass wanted to know, and Scooby said, when? There hadn't been a sleep for a few weeks, so she hadn't fallen asleep, no way. "She was just here on Friday, you idiot!"

But Mrs. Kogan stopped coming to school and Rorkisha said she heard that she had run off with Mr. Lavin, the gym teacher, that they loaded up his RV and took off for Branson or California. "Cause what the hell they gonna do, anyway? They gonna be asleep forever one of these months," Rorkisha said darkly. "They might as well have themselves a good time, right?"

Glass nodded dully, because he didn't like to think about it in those terms. A bunch of kids had stopped coming to school, too: Melissa, Dana, Somerson, fat Melissa. Mostly the white kids. Had their parents also left town? Where had they gone? To visit their grandparents? To Disneyland?

"They gone," Rorkisha said, grinning like a skull, grinning like one of his father's skulls in the old basement. "They ain't coming back. They gone."

One day, when school seemed nearly voluntary, Glass and Scooby skipped. No one but an old lady substitute teacher had been taking attendance and all they did all day was solve math problems on purple-inked dittos while Mrs. Gadsten or Miss Large did word search puzzles at the front of the room. What was the point of going to school?

Scooby had brought his father's gun. It gleamed blackly in his knapsack next to a box of bullets. "You sure he won't know you took it?" Glass asked, and Scooby said, "No way. He's working. He keeps it in an old boot and he never checks on it."

So they bicycled to Glass's old house.

It smelled musty and strange, the damp from the once-flooded basement rising up and infecting the first floor. The power had gone out a month ago and something—mice?—had gotten into one of the cabinets and eaten packets of peanut butter and cheese crackers. When Glass turned on the faucet, it gurgled a bit before the water began to flow.

It took Glass a few minutes to find a flashlight, and they descended the stairs carefully.

The basement felt damp now, and the legs of his father's desk were stained white from the flooding. The skulls eyed them from their shelves, strange and dark, black eyeholes, unhinged jaws.

"Dang," Scooby said, holding the flashlight, playing it over the old bones. "I thought you were exaggerating about all this."

Glass said nothing. He was remembering that night months ago now, standing ankle deep in water, inexplicably holding one of those skulls and weeping because he had nowhere to go and no future and no idea how to get through the night. And he was remembering his own father working at that desk, artifacts laid out in plastic trays while he carefully recorded their information on hand-drawn maps of fields outside town, or downriver at Chillicothe, or even Spring Ridge, which was near Arkansas. How he stood there one night and just watched his father make notes, then ran his fingers over the skulls, the gray boxes full of potsherds and flint flakes and scrapers and cores. How the basement smelled then of old bones and dust and of his father, of Old Spice and snuff.

Memories like that made him wince. His place was on Cora's sofa now, at Cora's little Formica kitchen table while she had a quick drink before heading off for work.

"One for the road," she would say, smiling at him and patting him on the back or rumpling his hair. "One for the road. Be good now."

They loaded four skulls into Scooby's knapsack—"They hardly weigh anything," Scooby said—and they bicycled down to Pertle Lake, then down the dirt paths to the far side of the lake where no one ever went, where once a road had been before they moved the route to downtown three decades ago.

They lined the skulls up on a rotting picnic table and, one by one, they took aim and shot, and mostly missed. But when they hit, the skulls exploded into fragments of glittering bone, some of the shards rising into the air in ways that seemed to Glass like slow motion. Over and over, a splinter of bone turned as it rose into the sun-dappled air.

"Damn," Scooby said, "that Indian just blew *up*!" and he laughed merrily and took another shot and missed, the bullet plunking pointlessly into an abandoned firepit.

+

In the fields all around town, the Indians slept. They had built the mounds that two hundred years of plows had leveled. They had walked the paths that the housing developments now covered. Their lives were under the BI-LO parking lot, under the sidewalks, under the tennis courts at Pertle Lake. Their bones were bright and cool in the cool deep earth. Theirs was the deepest possible sleep.

+

The location is secure, the young men and women working in the Sleepmobiles would say now. We are taking your loved one to a secure location where people will attend them. We are taking your loved one to a facility. Your loved one will be nourished and looked after, will be attended to by trained professionals, will be cared for. But at this time, we cannot tell you exactly which facility, we cannot be sure. The facilities are vast and the resources are vaster. And here is your paperwork. Please sign here and here. And here is a tracking number. If you will wait a week, if you will wait two weeks, and then call this number and give them your tracking information, they should be able to provide more information.

But the phone number was usually busy, and when it wasn't busy, the tracking information was usually confused, useless.

Some mentioned the vast construction projects outside Columbia and Maryville. Those were certainly facilities meant to contain more sleepers, vast bunkers, vaster piles of rubble and dirt and brick and stacked lumber. If not that, then what?

Others mentioned the empty hotels along the highway into Kansas City or around the airport. "I mean, there are so many empty beds in those places. They might as well use them. No one else is, probably."

The television wasn't helping, the anchors cheerful and upbeat about progress, progress, hopeful study results and prominent researchers in sleep studies, in sleep sicknesses, promising news from England, from Denmark, from China, and in other news . . .

Still others mentioned pillars of smoke rising from the low brick buildings near Osage Bluff. They'd never seen pillars of smoke there, coming from those defunct factory chimneys.

+

It had been Scooby's idea to line those skulls up and shoot them.

Scooby's mother was quarreling with his father again—he stayed out too late, Scooby told Glass—and she was exhausted from chasing kids around all day. *Exhausted*, she said. And she *still* had lessons to plan and a mess of second graders to worry about, some of them not yet even reading. And she'd been up too early, hadn't gotten any sleep at *all*, and what did Scooby know about work?

Not much. Scooby sat on the living room floor with his Atari joystick in his hand thinking about those skulls in Glass's basement, the rows of them. Glass had described them so vividly—Glass could tell a story, which is something Scooby admired—and Scooby wanted to see the skulls, and then he wanted to shoot the skulls.

He knew how to shoot—every boy in town knew how to shoot,

every boy but Glass. There were shooting ranges and there was deer season. During deer season, they canceled school for a week, and still Glass didn't know how to shoot. But Scooby could show him. Mr. Franklin had taken Scooby to the shooting range more than once. Scooby could teach Glass something *again*, because Scooby was always teaching Glass something. Yes, he was. And how *boss* to be shooting skulls and not bottles, skulls and not targets. They were gonna shoot that shit *up*.

But afterward, Glass had seemed—Scooby didn't have a word for it. Remote? There on the living room with his Atari, Scooby tried to understand his best friend.

Glass had been thinking about how his father had excavated those skulls from a nine-hundred-year-old Indian cemetery, how he'd cleaned them and plotted their burial locations and made notes about them in his notebook and written, in careful, indelible ink, specifications right there on the crania. It felt disrespectful.

It had been fun to fire the gun, but the image of that fragment of bone rising and spinning in the sun-dappled air stayed with him. And the shatter of bones on the rotted picnic table when they were through. And the smell of gunpowder. And Scooby leaping around, so excited.

"We shouldn't of done that," he said to Scooby when they were through, but Scooby never understood why. They were just skulls. No one got hurt, right?

+

The pillars of smoke rose from the low brick buildings far from the highways, far from the business district. The green-and-yellow vans backed up to the loading docks and stayed there while young men unloaded their cargoes.

The men who worked there laughed a lot and joked about the cargo, which had already grown cool and pale. What else could they do but joke about it. There was nothing else to be done. Dead weight. Corpsicle. They were well paid, after all. They were paid to do this job and not talk about it, not even to their girlfriends or mothers.

It was a kind of emergency work. It was like during wartime.

+

In early 1985 Cora made two decisions. First, she needed to find Jimbo, whoever he was. She still had no idea, even after searching Jake's car, even after the debacle at Jake's sister's house. She was at a dead end.

Second, she needed to clear the air with her sister, and the only way to do that was to drive to Omaha and confront her, to apologize, to fall, as it were, on her sword. The world was falling to pieces and it was ridiculous of Susan to be angry with her, ridiculous to be so angry—even if Cora had flirted with her husband, even if she had gone further than that, even if she had almost burned the place down. On balance, she'd still been a good younger sister, hadn't she? Yes, she had. For many years. She had been very good, except for this one thing. Except for these two things.

"Who's Jimbo," Glass asked, while Cora stirred the spaghetti pot.

"I don't know," Cora said. "That's the thing. I don't know. But, you know, I need those pills. You will, too, someday. I mean, if this . . . situation only gets worse."

"I know."

Glass skipped school again that day. He and Scooby had wandered around the edges of Pertle Lake and Scooby had found a fossil fern. Glass's mind was on that. On that particular species of fern.

"Jimbo," said Glass, absently, sitting at the kitchen table thinking of the fern. "Jim," Glass said, "bo."

Cora salted the pasta water. The grocery store was strangely stocked those days. The produce section was as good as ever, but the milk was tinned and sweetened. It was impossible to find soy sauce, but for some reason, there were vast quantities of pasta and jarred pasta sauce. So Cora, who never liked to cook, had focused on those.

"Jimbo," she said.

"So," said Glass, who was perched at the Formica kitchen table, quietly shredding a paper napkin, "is Bo like his last name? Or is it just one name? Is it, like, *Jimbo* or *Jim Bo*."

And that got Cora to thinking, because maybe she'd been wrong in her assumptions. Maybe it *was* Jim Bo, though what on earth kind of crazy last name was *Bo*?

But when she flipped through the local phone book, she found no Jim Bo, no Jim Boh, nothing like it.

Later, at the public library, she looked through the Kansas City phone book, the Lee's Summit phone book, the Overland Park phone book. Nothing. But in the Lone Jack phone book there was a James Beaux on Cannon Drive, a half-hour away.

"What do you think?" she asked Glass the next evening.

Glass said, "I don't think he's going to just give it to you."

+

When her brain split in two, when the Eight heated up her veins and made her dizzy, when it made her head pulse, she found herself increasingly in distant places. One part of her was in her living room, was in the doorway of the Black Walnut, was in the gray Datsun pulled to the side of the road. But another part of her was altogether elsewhere, was sometimes even in the distant past, back, for instance, when she was a little girl. She was a little girl again. Her mother and her mother's boyfriend had taken her and her sister to a baseball game at Municipal University. Why a baseball game? It didn't matter. Cora disliked the boyfriend and she disliked baseball and she hated that Susan was behaving so perfectly, was so perfectly friendly to all this, to this boyfriend and his big hands and his hairy arms and his sports, so she'd just left them all there on the bleachers. And then she was under the bleachers, wandering around in the shade beneath the bleachers, and it occurred to her that this was a good place to be, that the people above might drop things from their pockets and they'd fall all the way down here, where she was, and she scanned the ground as she walked, the noise of the baseball game around her, the loudspeaker and the cheers, and sure enough she found a quarter, and another quarter. And then a dollar bill. And a baseball cap. All kinds of things that the people seated high above her had lost.

That image crystallized for her as the Eight heated up her veins, as the Eight pressed down upon her, a memory of the baseball game, her mother's short-term boyfriend, and leaning over and picking up that dollar bill that had fallen from someone's pocket high above.

Then the simultaneity converged onto the present moment and Cora came back into her singular self, wherever she happened to be, in the Black Walnut, in the car, or in the kitchen. The sirens had stopped ringing. The town was asleep and would stay that way for ten, fifteen, maybe twenty minutes.

+

Why did it have to be so *racial*, she wondered. It wasn't fair, it wasn't fair. She wasn't a prejudiced person. She was no racist. Years ago, when she passed Black people in the grocery store, on the street, she didn't think too much about them. Oh, perhaps if she looked closely into herself she might have discovered the smallest wariness there, or guilt, a quick hesitation mixed with nervousness, a sense of her own skin.

Because here was someone who was less fortunate than she was, someone who, perhaps faultless, was held back. Someone who didn't have the same access she had had to excellent schools, to coaches and good teachers. Someone who could never win the Nebraska statewide diving competition or turn down a spot at Stanford for a full ride at Nebraska, someone who might have all kinds of invisible hardships.

It wasn't that she felt superior—though there was maybe a little of that, if she examined herself closely—but that she wanted to help, to be a friend, to be a white friend. To lift someone up. Not that she had ever gotten to know anyone to lift up. She hadn't. She didn't really know Black people well, though she told herself she wasn't against the idea.

Now, when she passed one of them in the street, when she waited on one of them at the Black Walnut, she felt momentarily a pang of despair for herself. They could laugh and drink their beer and eat their curly fries with a near certainty that Cora never again could have.

Seeing this, she felt not rage—though she knew some people who harbored rage, for sure, had heard about the rage in Kansas City, in St. Louis, the violent rage, but hadn't seen it here, not yet, though it was here. Instead she felt a kind of sadness, and her hand would involuntarily touch the little bottle that held her decreasing supply of Eight.

"Can I take your order," she'd say to the Black couple sitting by the window at the Black Walnut. And they'd scrutinize the menu for a moment or ask a question about a drink.

She'd take their order, feeling inside her a mixture of love and relief, discomfort and something she didn't want to call resentment.

+

"I'm going to drive to Omaha to visit my sister," she told Glass, "and I'm going to talk to James Beaux."

Glass put down the horror novel he'd taken from Cora's shelf, a novel about an airplane haunted by evil spirits. Would there be airplanes in the future?

He'd been fidgety all day, riding his bike and sitting on the sofa, flipping through the unchanging television networks—Cora couldn't afford cable, she'd said—picking up and putting down the novel. He'd even been to school, where he'd sat at his desk and failed to solve several math problems that Miss Large failed to bother to grade.

"You have a sister?" he said. He thought he knew everything about her. He knew where she'd gone to school, he knew she wrote plays and sometimes stories and poems. He had, in fact, read several of them. There was one poem about a flock of birds rising up from the surface of a pond late one fall. They rose "like a great black net," and now whenever Glass saw the flocks of blackbirds or starlings rising above the BI-LO parking lot, he thought about nets. And he'd read another poem about laundry falling through the laundry chute, down, down into the basement. The laundry, she said, was like the soul of the house, moving, falling, invisible, between the walls. He'd had one of those little laundry chute doors in his own bedroom and when he was very little, he'd dropped Hot Wheels cars into it, hearing them land on the dark concrete basement floor far below.

Also a play about a man who was a human cannonball at the circus, but he wanted to quit, he wanted someone else to be the human cannonball, to be fired out of the cannon into the great net, but no one else wanted that job. No one, and the human cannonball had no choice but to continue with his line of work or starve.

And a play about a cryogenically frozen man whose defrosted head sat on a table and sang songs about the days of old while the people of the future tried to make sense of his memories of the past, of his grocery stores and video arcades.

The truth was, when Cora was away and Glass wasn't otherwise occupied, he made a study of her things, going through her desk drawers, her dresser, looking at her old high school ID, fingering her library card. He read around in her books, especially the passages she'd highlighted, the stories she'd photocopied, the poems on dogeared pages. He'd held her diving medals and her diplomas and read the aborted drafts of the openings of plays she never finished, because she was stuck, stuck, stuck, she couldn't write anything, she was blocked. He'd gone through her photo albums, had looked at pictures of her diving, snapshots of her and her friends playing Putt-Putt golf, playing tennis, lying under a tree with a tray of cupcakes. He'd seen the Polaroids of someone who might have been her mother or an aunt, a pretty, narrow-faced woman, her hair pulled back into a ponytail. Then more pictures of friends. Was one of those friends actually her sister?

"You'll be OK on your own, right? I mean, you'll get off to school or whatever you do?" Cora was saying, but Glass was thinking about her sister.

"I didn't know you had a sister," Glass said. "You never talk about her."

"It's complicated," Cora said.

"Can I come?" he asked. He wanted to meet her sister. He wanted to spend two days in the car with Cora.

"Not a chance," Cora said.

+

When she said it, he looked almost unbearably sad, and she'd meant to say something to soften it, something kind. She considered Glass to be a little obsessive, a little strange. She knew he'd been into her things. She didn't mind too much, though. No one else takes an interest, she thought, and if he was looking at her notebooks and photo albums, well, what did it matter? At least someone cared about her, at least she was important to someone.

And if he was sneaking into her horror novels—she loved horror novels, wholly and unironically—if he was sneaking into her horror novels, that also meant he was reading, right? And that was a good thing, with school being so spotty and her not exactly having the time to be his teacher on top of everything else. She had hidden a couple of the really inappropriate ones where he wouldn't find them, the ones about zombie cannibals, the one called *Scalps*.

He had looked so stung when she'd told him he couldn't come. He'd gotten up and left the room and she'd found him a little while later sitting on the apartment's front steps pretending that all was cool, yeah, sure, he could stay there alone. She had nothing to worry about.

But she did worry. Because he really was just a kid. Eleven or twelve? She didn't even know how old. Why didn't she know how old? Anyway, he was a kid.

+

Even Glass knew that the trip to Omaha was not safe. Not these days. Not for a woman alone. He'd heard the stories like everyone else. Stories of lawlessness as the sleeps increased, a sense that one was somehow beyond punishment, that the punishment looming in the future—the final punishment—was so great that nothing inflicted by earthly authority was worth much consideration.

Skipping school, shooting up those skulls were just small manifestations of a much larger shift and he could not forget Rorkisha snapping her gum by the water fountain, going on about her cousin Rita, whom she didn't much like, thank you, how her cousin Rita got tied up behind the Chickasaw Trucks lot by three white guys who flicked burning matches at her and put out their cigarettes on her arms and laughed and sprayed whipped cream in her hair and then just left her there where the ants crawled all over her head. No one much cared about Rita, Rorkisha said. Not the police nor anyone else. Not one bit, and she had to free herself and had the rope burns on her wrists to prove it.

Here Rorkisha paused dramatically and arched one eyebrow. "I don't like her none," she said, "but I don't wish that on her."

Then suddenly she looked actually shaken—Rorkisha, who was unflappable, who could stare anyone down, fierce Rorkisha Cattlidge—she bowed her head and shook it back and forth. And Glass saw her wipe away a tear. He saw it, so he knew it had happened. Rorkisha Cattlidge was crying.

"I'm sorry," he'd said. "I'm sorry about Rita."

"She's all right," said Rorkisha. "You get out of my face now, please."

Glass was thinking about this back at Pertle Lake, where he gathered the fragments of the Indian skulls and dropped them in a white plastic garbage bag, one fragment after the other, searching the ground for even the smallest slivers. One after the other, until he'd found every bit of skull.

Then he carried that bag over by the lakeside, where he'd dug a hole with one of his father's spades. And he dropped that bag in the hole and covered it up with dirt. And on top of the little mound, he dropped the biggest rock he could carry from the lake bank, a pink-and-white granite boulder. It must have weighed fifty pounds.

+

At Scooby's house, later that day, they'd played Crystal Castles and Pitfall! and Galaxian on the Atari. Scooby's mother brought them red Jell-O and then disappeared into the kitchen again. She looked exhausted but, in Glass's opinion, so pretty, her full face and dark eyes and long, slender fingers. Glass always noticed beauty. He was, without knowing it, a sort of connoisseur of beauty, and his eyes lingered on Mrs. Franklin's cheekbones, her fine hands, and then they returned to Crystal Castles on the TV screen, retaining the memory of Mrs. Franklin.

When Scooby went off to the bathroom, Glass slipped quietly into Mrs. Franklin's bedroom, then into the closet, among the rows of shoes and sandals, and there in the back of the closet, a pair of heavy work boots. He reached inside. There was the paper lunch bag, the gun, the half-empty box of bullets. Quickly, he slipped these into his knapsack and almost made it back to the Atari when Scooby appeared by the bathroom door.

"What're you doing in my parents' bedroom?" he asked.

The hallway was dark and narrow and Glass could see the TV's glow in the living room, could hear the quick bright Atari video game music.

"Nothing," said Glass.

"Oh," said Scooby, looking at him strangely. "I mean—"

"I just didn't know where you'd gone," Glass said. "You just took off, so I was looking for you."

"I was in the bathroom, you idiot," said Scooby, laughing. "The bathroom. That's my parents' bedroom."

"Yeah, sorry," Glass said, and they returned to the video game, which was making upbeat, pulsing, harpsichord-like music in the living room.

"You boys all right?" said Mrs. Franklin from the kitchen where she was chopping onions and carrots.

"We good," said Scooby.

The gun was heavy as a lie in Glass's knapsack.

7 JIM BEAUX

No one answered the door at James Beaux's house in Lone Jack, but Cora didn't want to drive the thirty minutes back home.

Instead she drove around the little downtown, then parked in front of a ratty restaurant that called itself Oriental Cuisine, though it had clearly once been a gas station. The windows were greasy and a torn pink awning flapped in the wind.

She lingered for a while in her car, revising an opening scene in her mind, something she'd been working fruitlessly on for a week or two. Everything she wrote these days was garbage, garbage. The radio played REO Speedwagon, then Foreigner. She couldn't get past the first scene of anything, anything, anything. Every idea she had fell flat, every character she thought up became useless, untenable, and, worst of all, boring. She had tried and tried and was trying now.

She tilted the seat back and closed her eyes and shifted the opening dialogue to the back of the scene, and opened with something else. Then she mentally refigured the part of the plot that took place at a gas station, a threatening young man confronting a confused woman who was looking for her lost child. But the scene wasn't right. It wouldn't work.

The spring air was cold and brisk and she could tell, walking now, that it would soon rain. At the laundromat, two sallow girls sat on the curb looking at their yellow shoes. The great dryers turned and she could smell detergent.

She stopped before the Lone Jack Historical Society and Public Library, which she had heard had once been a mattress store. Or was it a dime store? She looked through the window, then entered the musty building. Someone had moved in a few oak and glass cases and filled them with arrowheads, early photographs, postcards, a Civil War belt buckle, an old pair of silver spurs, a display of fossil ferns. Someone had hung photographs and early maps of Lone Jack on the walls and posted a Timeline of Life in Lone Jack going all the way back to 1841. A cigar-store Indian stood by a drinking fountain in the back of the room and two walls held floor-to-ceiling metal bookshelves lined with paperbacks and Book-of-the-Month hardbacks. One wall of shelves was labeled simply Nonfiction, the other Fiction.

Once, Cora and her sister and two boys whose names she didn't remember had spent the night in a shabby little museum just like this at Eastern Nebraska State College, where her sister had gone for two years, before dropping out and getting married.

It had begun as a sort of joke—to slip into the three-room museum before closing. They'd brought a couple bottles of Southern Comfort, and they'd stayed up all night drinking and talking and wandering among the display cases. One dusty old case held an actual Aztec mummy and Cora wondered what that mummy would have thought, had it known it would someday be sleeping under glass in Garson, Nebraska, and one of the boys even lifted the case's Plexiglas lid and reached inside, caressing the mummy's black leathery face, laughing drunkenly. "It feels like hard plastic," he'd said, his hand on the mummy's exposed cheek, on its ear, and then a bit of its nose fell off into his palm and the boy held it up like a trophy and they'd laughed and laughed, and then he'd drunkenly tried to push the fragment back into the mummy's black face, but that didn't work, and it fell to the side of its cheek.

Cora had brought a little pot, which they smoked among the artifacts; even her sister had tried it. The mummy slept and slept and how she had loved her sister then. How she had loved her, through the haze of smoke, Susan, whom everyone liked because she was good and funny and quick to joke, because it had been her idea to hide out in that little campus museum. And when the sun finally rose, the four of them slipped out, still drunk and fuzzy and bone-tired, and staggered back to the dormitories, and Susan crawled into her own bed, and Cora, who was only visiting for the weekend, crawled in next to her, and the two of them slept in that bed for five hours.

"Can I help you?" a stout woman with glasses asked.

"Oh, I was just looking around," said Cora.

The woman nodded. The cigar-store Indian in the corner looked blankly toward the door.

+

Now a rusted blue station wagon was parked in the driveway at James Beaux's ranch house, so she knocked again, three times, holding her umbrella awkwardly, but the old man who answered the door in an undershirt that strained over his belly said there wasn't no James Beaux here. Not these last six months, anyway.

"I'm living here now, me and my two girls. James Beaux just plumb left this place and moved t'other side of town in one of them McMansions they got by Jones Park and he give this house to me. He give it to me flat out, 'cause he don't have no use for a little house like this. But he come around here time and again to get his mail and see who's looking for him. So who're you?"

"Do you know which house?"

"The big green'un," the man said, scratching his belly. His undershirt was stained a kind of green. Green Jell-O, Cora thought.

When she found the only green McMansion by Jones Park, it was already getting dark. And cold. It felt like snow, though it was already March. The house was large and faux Victorian with two green turrets and a vast Southern-style front porch, painted white. A white porch swing dangled and shifted gently in the wind. It must have been the largest house in town. A Porsche 911 sat in the driveway.

The man who came to the door was young and skinny, in pleated chinos and a powder-blue Ocean Pacific windbreaker. He smiled and Cora stepped back a bit. His teeth were bright white and large, his face narrow, his hair blond and cut quite short and feathered. "Can I help you?" he asked.

He was not at all what Cora had expected. She had expected someone rough, someone who lived in a trailer, not a young man in a green mansion with a Porsche 911 in the driveway.

But he was James Beaux, of course he was, he said. And yeah, he knew Jake Petersen, how was Jake doing these days? Oh, asleep? I'm so sorry. All them poor sleeping souls, them poor sleeping souls. Why, he hadn't heard from Jake in months, so it wasn't exactly a surprise, things being as they are, but he was sorry to have it confirmed. "How can I help you?" he said again.

Cora had gone over and over her script—a script that involved her gently cajoling James Beaux (if James Beaux was, in fact, Jimbo) into acknowledging that he was, in fact, the source of Jake's Eight Track, and then cajoling him further into selling some to her, perhaps trading some for Jake's car, perhaps telling her where she could get more, perhaps, perhaps. But faced with him now—his blinding teeth, his easy manner, his smooth country accent—all she could say was, "I'm wondering about acquiring some Eight Track."

"Eight?" the young man said.

Cora nodded.

The young man laughed. "I don't have any Eight," he said. He had come out onto the porch now.

"But Jake said—"

The young man looked at her for a moment, then another, as if quietly taking her measure, as if adding up all her features and seeing what they equaled. At last he said, "Look, I once had a lot of Eight, back when it was new and you could get it, and Jake and a few other guys sold some of it on commission along with a few other items I used to deal in, but no one has Eight Track anymore. That was last year. There isn't any Eight no more, not for the likes of you or me."

"None?" Cora said softly.

"If you're super rich, maybe," the young man said, looking over her shoulder to the old Datsun in the driveway. "But I don't guess you're rich. Ain't that Jake's car?"

"I'm not rich," Cora said.

"Neither am I," James said. "I only recently moved in here after I sold what Eight I could spare, a couple bottles. The rest ain't for sale."

"No one's selling?" she said again, feeling her knees shake.

"No one."

"Not for anything?"

"Not since the sleeps went past three minutes and everyone got serious," he said. He was still smiling, but his smile looked pasted on, like a smile cut from a toothpaste ad and glued to his face.

"No one at all," she said, not as a question but as a kind of statement.

Behind her, a cold wind rippled through the black oak trees. The young man's smile faded.

"Look, sorry," he said. "Production is slow and the labs have all been taken over by"—he gestured sweepingly, as if taking in the whole United States—"I don't know who. No one asked me. I'd like to say it's the government, but I don't know." He sighed, his hands deep in his pockets. The white porch swing swung back and forth, creaking in the cool air.

“The rich will survive,” he continued, “if they can survive the Eight. It messes up your brain, you know.”

She stared at him dumbly.

“They’ll survive, and fuck everyone else,” he said. “Same old story, right?”

+

Same old story, same old story, same old story rattling through her mind as she drove, rattling along to the radio’s innocuous fizz of pop music, of girl bands and advertisements for cigarettes and used cars and hamburgers, as if she should just keep on going, hoping that the sleeps would stop, that the scientists would develop a cure beyond Eight Track, that the scientists could cure the weather that swept and swept and swept into town. It was snowing now, bright white flakes swirling in the night, swirling in the headlights’ glare, swirling and vanishing so quickly. Could she divide the pills in two? Might she have double the doses? She was petite, and Jake, who must have been twice her weight, had taken a tablet only once and stayed awake, drowsily, through a two-minute sleep. She would divide the pills in two, she thought, feeling the panic in her fingers, which were drumming on the steering wheel as she drove Highway 50 back toward town and the snow swirled over the windshield, a late, wet snow. *Same old story, same old story*, James had said, and he was right and there was nothing she could do about it.

I can tell you here that she was right, there was nothing she could have done about it, nothing at all. No Eight Track would be hers, because what Eight there was, and what Eight there *would be*, was now carefully controlled, was doled out only to those people who were essential, who were vital to the survival of the state, or it was traded underground, was fought for and sold far beyond her means, and there could be no more Eight for a waitress who lived in the middle of nowhere, even if she was also a pretty good writer, even if she had turned down Stanford for the University of Nebraska, even if she was taking care of a kid who was basically an orphan and she had a good heart—she was a *good* person, though her only family member wasn't speaking to her and sometimes she stole small things from shops just to feel the thrill in her bones. There could be no Eight for her just as there would have been no Eight for you or for me, had we been alive there, at that particular time in that early spring of 1985.

+

She parked the car on West Pine Street in the light of the bars and the throb of the jukeboxes, got out wearily, and the full awfulness, the unrelenting awfulness of her situation filled her. The tight rope trembled, she thought, and showed the darkness beneath—a line recollected inaccurately from a book she once loved, a book by a doomed author who died pointlessly and alone. "The tight rope trembled," she said out loud as she climbed the dark stairs to her apartment, kicking snow off of her loafers, wiping it out of her hair.

When she unlocked the door she found the living room full of light and noise and Glass was sitting cross-legged on the floor in front of the television. She heard the high trill of computerized music and there he was playing Galaxia or Galaga or whatever it was called, totally absorbed, moving the joystick and firing, click-click-click, until three musical notes descended in defeat and the screen flashed Game Over, Game Over, Game Over, and "Where have you been?" Glass asked. "I thought you weren't working tonight. I thought we were going to play video games."

+

Earlier that day, Scooby had wanted to go back to Glass's old house, to look at those skulls. "And whatever other cool shit you've got in the basement," he'd added, and Glass had tried to demur.

“C’mon,” Scooby said. “We don’t have to shoot up any skulls. I just want to see what else is down there. It’s cool,” he said. “You *know* it is.”

They were at Cora’s apartment, and Scooby was looking the place over, having never been there before.

“She’s, like, a teacher?” he asked.

“Yeah,” Glass said. “She used to be. Now she’s a waitress.”

“Oh,” said Scooby. “Right.” He picked up one of her books, turned it over, then put it back down distractedly.

Glass didn’t know where Cora was, but she’d taken the car and her bag and left no note.

Because Scooby’s mother taught second grade, Scooby almost always had to go to school in the morning, even though they hardly ever had a regular teacher anymore. Glass usually followed along and sat at his desk among the dwindling schoolchildren, and if they had a chance they’d slip away in the afternoon, which is what they had just done.

“Spooky,” said Scooby, looking around the dark kitchen. A mouse must have been chewing on an old copy of *Newsweek* on the kitchen counter. There were cracker wrappers on the floor. The aluminum flashlight glittered on the counter where Glass had left it. The air was cold—it was cold outside, too—and the smell of mold was strong on the basement stairs.

Scooby shone the light on the skulls and they grinned back meanly. “Damn,” he said, entranced. “Damn.”

The one with the hole above its eye glimmered in the light and Scooby reached out to touch it and Glass caught his breath, but didn’t say anything.

“All those dead Indians,” said Scooby.

“The boxes,” Glass said, “are mostly other kinds of bones and pieces of broken pots.” He hesitated. “But you can look inside them if you want.”

“Uh-huh,” said Scooby, unable to look away from the skulls.

It was true, everyone was falling asleep but these people had *died*, these people had gone that extra little bit into pure oblivion and had been buried and grieved for and moldered in the dirt before Missouri was Missouri, before cornfields were cornfields, and Scooby just stared, entranced, trying to understand it in all its vastness, until Glass said, “Look, I’ve gotta check something out upstairs.”

“Uh-huh,” said Scooby.

Glass went upstairs and sat on the old sofa, the one he and his father had sat on together for years and years, his whole life, really. He picked up the remote control and aimed it at the cable box, at the TV, and pressed the button. Nothing. Nothing. Just darkness, the late-afternoon light filtering in through the windows.

He walked around the living room, the dining room, the bathroom, fingering things that were familiar to him, familiar from another life, a little bronze bird his father had told him was very old, a coffee cup with a grinning Cheshire cat, a half-empty can of Copenhagen snuff, his father’s blue slippers, right where he’d kicked them off by the bathroom scale.

+

He had planned to give her the gun for her trip to Omaha. He knew from horror movies that she might need it. But that evening when she had come in wet from snow, when she had brushed it out of her hair and slung her colorful, wet Guatemalan bag over the side of the sofa, she sat down heavily and looked at him. He couldn’t tell what she was thinking, what she was feeling. Her face was entirely blank, and she looked into his eyes not with any particular tenderness, but as if she was trying to figure something out. And Glass looked right back at her, because what else could he do?

The video game was still flashing Game Over, Game Over and would continue indefinitely.

She looked him up and down and sighed and said at last, "So, you want to go to Omaha?"

He looked back at her, because the moment felt serious, though he didn't know why. At last he said Yes, he would like to go to Omaha. He would really like to go to Omaha.

"Then you should pack up," she said, "because we're leaving tomorrow."

Glass knew his heart should be singing because his own town was nothing, because he didn't care anymore about those kids who parked their cars in the BI-LO parking lot and listened to throbbing music, and the movie theater was only showing old movies these days, movies he'd seen two years ago, or movies starring no one he had ever heard of, lame versions of *Star Wars* with obvious puppets and visible strings holding up the spaceships. They were so laughable. His heart should be singing because he'd have four hours in the car with Cora each way, because maybe they'd stay in a hotel—were there still hotels? Of course there were!—but he felt, instead, a little bit somber.

Cora's face was a mask. She didn't try to smile. "We'll leave tomorrow," she said. "Pack warm clothes and extra socks, OK? And don't forget your toothbrush and other crap."

Anyway, he had planned to give her the gun, but now he didn't have to. He'd just keep it nearby. He'd keep it handy.

Everyone in town had a gun, Scooby had told him once, surprised that Glass had, until that time, never fired one. Some folks got two, three, ten, a hundred guns, Scooby said. But Cora didn't have a gun, and Glass had a feeling she wouldn't want one around. Best not to give it to her, but to pack it with his things, just in case.

He could hear her in the next room, talking into the phone. "Hi," she was saying, "uh, hi. Susan. It's Cora. Look, you haven't answered my messages so, uh, I don't know what to think of that. But I'm coming home. I, uh, hope I can see you."

+

Here is what Cora was thinking when she looked at Glass: Could she leave him here for a day, maybe two days, maybe three? Could she drive him to his friend Scooby's house and just leave him there? Could she just walk away from him? No, she thought, no, and no.

He was hers now. She was responsible. She'd never been responsible for anyone but herself, and she'd messed that up so catastrophically that, well, how could she be responsible for this kid whose age she didn't even know, whose story she understood only vaguely, who disappeared for hours and hours, then sat on her sofa reading the same books over and over again? She could not, she could not. But she couldn't get rid of him, either. There was nothing for her to do.

He was a good kid. She liked him. And she had not expected that. And she had not been ready for him.

He had looked up from his Atari, disappointed, and said, "I thought we were going to play video games."

And she'd looked back at him. It would have been nice to sit around and play video games. She would have liked, in a perfect world, to have a little brother, a little son, someone to be responsible for. "So you want to go to Omaha?" she had said abruptly. And he had looked at her blankly at first, utterly blank. And then, after a moment, he had said yes, but he'd said it as if it were a question.

"Yes?"

+

That night Glass lay awake in bed thinking about Carlos's wasps. In his imagination, they had never moved on from their various aquariums, from the moonscape and the Christmas diorama and the Swiss Alps. In his imagination the wasps had multiplied, their papery nests filling the aquariums, the garage overwhelmed by them, rising and falling, buzzing stupidly in the dark, crawling the plastic tunnels from one aquarium to the next, thousands of wasps, the incessant hum of them, until Glass could hardly stand it and covered his ears because of their noise, because of the wasps crawling over Shane's green Chevrolet, crawling over the tops of Carlos's aquariums, crawling out through the garage door cracks, rising into the rich Missouri afternoon light, a stream of wasps, wasps like thin plumes of smoke.

Then Cora was shaking him awake because, "Time to get up, Glass. Rise and shine, Glass. You all packed? You got your toothbrush, you got your underwear and shoes and socks, you got your *Microvac* book?"

Yes, yes, yes, he had all that. And the gun, too, stuffed in the corner of his little duffel bag, wrapped in a pair of Wranglers.

8 TO OMAHA . . .

When Scooby came by Cora's apartment a few days later, when he climbed the stairs and pounded on the door and, again, heard nothing inside, he did what he told himself he wouldn't do, he shouldn't do, until he was sure something was wrong. He lifted the worn-out green welcome mat as Glass had done a week ago and found the key and he unlocked the door and let himself in.

The apartment was lit only by the afternoon streaming through the windows, settling on the furniture.

Scooby called out, "Yo, Glass! Glass," pointlessly and fruitlessly, because it was obvious neither Glass nor Cora was there.

He looked around the living room. The Atari lay on the floor, useless brown and black plastic. The sofa Glass slept on was empty, his blanket rumpled into a ball on the floor. The kitchen was clean, a few dishes in the drying rack, a half-empty bottle of wine sitting near the sink. A bag of brown rice on the counter beside a measuring cup.

On Cora's bed a few T-shirts had been laid out flat, considered and rejected. Scooby ran his fingers over them. Blondie and Cheap Trick, concert T-shirts. Earrings in a box on the dresser, a black leather wristband with the letter *C* stamped into it. It was the absence of toothbrushes and toothpaste in the bathroom that told Scooby that Cora and Glass had gone somewhere, had packed up and taken off.

When the power failed the day before, the phone lines had gone down, too, so Glass couldn't have called if he wanted to. Couldn't have called, could not call. If he was even alive. If they were alive.

Scooby sat heavily on the edge of Cora's bed and looked out the window onto West Pine, weirdly deserted now, though it was mid-afternoon. After a moment he saw someone walking down the middle of the road pushing a shopping cart filled with empty beer mugs. What was he going to do with those? Scooby thought, but the man just rattled on down the street, singing loudly and incoherently, pushing his shopping cart within which the beer mugs clinked and chimed.

+

Scooby locked up Cora's apartment and slipped the key back under the doormat and walked heavily down the stairs to where he'd leaned his bicycle against the lamppost. But when he got there the bike was gone. Someone had ridden off with it. Why would anyone steal his bicycle now, now when the power was out, when the phones were out, when things were really bad, why would anyone steal his kid-size bicycle?

He looked up and down the street, the silent brick buildings, the rows of parking meters, the cracked sidewalks, and smalltown decay, Gluck Hardware, Hero's Bar, Jonny's T-Shirt Shop, the Donut Hole, Fitters, Java Junction, some doors, he learned later, jimmied open, their freezers emptied, the absolute worthlessness of this little town, its criminals, and Scooby stood there without his bicycle. He shook his head. The strange old guy with the shopping cart was back, the cart empty now, and he pushed it up over the curb and onto the sidewalk and disappeared inside Fitters Pub.

Scooby would have to walk home. And when he got home he'd have to face his father, who had told him absolutely not to venture into town. "Absolutely not, even to look for your friend, because you don't know what's going on right now, you don't know what those people are up to. They're crazy, y'hear? You stay with your mama and I'm just going to go see to the club, going to take home what I can and unlock the doors so people don't break the windows in—best just to unlock the doors—and you stay here and do what your mama says."

Scooby had stayed home for as long as he could, but finally he slipped away to check on Glass and only managed to get his bicycle stolen. So now he was walking home, past the nice two-story houses and their sleeping occupants, past the middle school and the BI-LO, and soon he'd be walking past Pertle Lake then over the tracks and into his half of town, the part of town he knew best—though in truth he knew the whole town backward and forward, had ridden every street with Glass on their bikes—back to the part of town that belonged to him, and to his own home, to his own father, who hated everything about the people who would break into Fitters Bar and steal their frozen steaks and steal their bottles of vodka and steal their beer mugs. His father who was, above all things, an honest man, and his mother, who was sitting on the edge of their bed crying.

"You got to look after your little sister," his father had said, "you gotta help out around here now and quit being silly. Because they not going to get any less crazy."

And all he'd managed to do was lose his bicycle.

+

Four days earlier, they'd thrown their bags into the trunk and driven up West Pine, then left on Maguire toward Business Route 13, the melting ice crunching under their wheels. Cora had turned on the radio and first it was the Go-Go's singing "Our Lips are Sealed," and Cora said, "I love this stupid song," and she sang along and Glass tried to sing along, too, but, though he knew the tune, he didn't know the words. The song was already pretty old. And then it was "Wake Me Up, Before You Go-Go," the DJ joking about how it was all *go, go, go*, yessiree, *go, go, go* here in Lone Jack and beyond! And the snow melted on the road and pretty soon they were on State Route 50 with its occasional farmhouses, its silos and gas stations, passing Lone Jack with James Beaux's ridiculous green Victorian house, his Porsche 911, zipping toward Lee's Summit and Highway 29, which was a real highway.

In the distance they saw the smoke rising from Osage Bluff, but they thought nothing of it. Osage Bluff, down by the train tracks, down by the reservoirs, black pillars of smoke, and they drove right by and onto Highway 29, no problems. The gun slept, comfortable as a child, wrapped in Glass's denim Wranglers.

"You got a favorite song?" Cora asked him finally, and Glass said that, yeah, he did. He had a few favorite songs, and one of them was "Come On Eileen" by Dexys Midnight Runners, and Cora nodded and said, "Good song," and Glass looked out the window and glowed. "Good song, good song," he said to himself, and half an hour later, amazingly, that very song came on the radio and Cora and Glass sang it together.

And Cora laughed and said the lyrics were pretty stupid, really, but the song was good pop, it was a good pop song, though she preferred Blondie, she preferred The Clash, she preferred The Jam, she preferred The Smiths, on and on, she preferred, she preferred. And that was just fine with Glass, who *preferred* with her, deep into the tunnel of songs and bands he had never heard of, bands he didn't know existed, bands he preferred because she preferred them as they drove past farmhouses and fields of cows all facing, mysteriously, the same way. And some nutjob had set up a kind of commune on his farm, a kind of gun cult, who knew what, signs all along his property, THE END IS NEAR, COME AND TAKE IT! and THE LORD ABIDES!, whatever that meant. "Fucking nuts," said Cora.

And pretty soon they were coming up on Nebraska City, then Bellevue, and Glass had never been happier in this life. Not ever.

+

The sign for the Steffins Equestrian Center and Stables was a shiny periwinkle blue, each letter carved deep into the wood and lacquered red or black. It was a handsome sign on two wooden posts sunk deep into the ground beside a long driveway that extended past a grove of apple trees to the stables and her sister's house. Cora was there when Richard made that sign in his woodshop, when he sanded it, painted it so carefully, then coated it with something milky that dried strong and glossy.

Then he'd dug two good deep holes while Cora leaned against a tree and watched him work and twice offered to help. Twice he'd let her hold the signposts while he strapped two levels to the sides with electrical tape and positioned them perfectly, before pouring in the cement.

At that moment, it was true, she'd wanted simply to touch his arm, to be near him, to inhale him, to touch someone mature, someone competent—not like her, not faking competence. Someone who could do useful things easily, who could mount that blue sign on those posts, knowing it wouldn't tip over or rot, who knew how much cement to mix and how deep to dig the holes and how to strap two levels to the side of each signpost to make sure it was perfect.

Now that sign was years old, but it looked new and she stopped the car for a moment to look at it, wet from a passing shower, and the old feeling washed over her for just a moment, a fragment of a moment, a feeling of yearning so quick it might have evaporated into nothing, and then Glass said, "Your sister lives at a stable?" and she pulled forward, down the long driveway, past the apple trees and the stables to the big blue two-story house.

Her sister's gray Volvo was right where it had always been, parked at the side of the house, next to Richard's pickup and the red-and-blue horse trailers. The stable wall had been repaired. It was just a little past noon and sun filtered through the canopy of oak trees, dappling the driveway. When she parked the car, when she stretched her legs, she noticed the tinkling of wind chimes, four sets of wind chimes running along the porch eave. The air smelled of grass, recent rain, hay, and horses, and that sense of being among family flooded Cora's every nerve, cell, and capillary, and she almost could have cried. She had been alone for so long, she had been waiting tables and hanging around in bars, feeling sorry for herself, and here she was. Here she was. She had no idea what to expect, if she would be welcome or not.

It was strange that the grass was long, that it came up over her shoes and to her shins in places. Funny that when she got closer to the porch, one of the wind chimes was not quite correct, but leaned weirdly to the side, a couple strings rotted through. But she was here, she had taken this step and she'd take another. She knocked on the door.

+

But the door did not open, not when she knocked again, louder, and again, and then suddenly it did open, and there was Susan in her bathrobe, having come perhaps from the shower, her long hair wet. She looked scrubbed and pink and, at the same time, tired, and she stood in the open doorway and looked at Cora and Glass without speech, her mouth partly open. She took a breath, and then another.

"I didn't know—" she said at last.

"I—" said Cora. She had, without thinking, drawn Glass close to her, had her arm on his shoulder.

Susan looked like she was trying to decide something, like she was trying to figure out what to say and how to say it. But then a kind of resolution crossed her face and she smiled and said, "I had no idea you were coming." The wind chimes tinkled around them and the broken one swayed limply in the breeze. "I had no idea," she said.

"But I called and called!"

"I'm sorry," she said. "We've been so busy here."

She invited them in, maybe a little reluctantly, and they sat at the kitchen table and Cora tried to explain about Glass, and now Susan smiled and said it didn't matter, it was OK that they had come. It was a welcome thing to have a child around the house. She made Cora coffee but had only Tab for Glass, warm in a glass with only one ice cube. The radio was playing the weather report over and over again, high of sixty-five degrees with scattered showers, lows tonight in the forties, so stay warm, stay warm.

Cora sipped her coffee and then suggested that Glass go outside for a bit, go and see the horses, and when he was gone, Cora said, "I'm so sorry, I'm so sorry," and Susan nodded and said, "Well, that is in the past, it is the past," but Cora wanted to talk about it, to explain herself, about what a failure she'd been, about how she had never wanted to mess things up so badly, but Susan just smiled and said, "Look, let's just get past it, OK?" because it had been a rotten few years, the whole thing was rotten and stupid.

And how was Richard, Cora wanted to know, and Susan said he was fine, he was doing well, he was over in the next county, something about buying a new mower for the horse trails, but he'd be along, though perhaps not before Cora had to head back home. She drummed her long fingers on the table as she said this, then sipped her tea.

That evening she defrosted steaks and rubbed them with salt and pepper and heated up the cast-iron skillet. She sprinkled the steaks with rosemary, humming to herself while Cora sat at the kitchen table talking about everything she'd been through, about losing her job at the university, about Jake and his car and the Eight Track and Glass showing up at her apartment—she couldn't just leave him there, after all.

After returning from the stables, Glass joined them in the kitchen and told Susan about his dad, and he talked about *The Microvac Chronicles*, how Amanda had just learned that the key to shutting down Microvac wasn't as easy as flipping a switch, but it involved, instead, closing down a mind, the vast mind of Microvac itself, Microvac a thinking, feeling being. It involved something closer to killing than turning off the lights, and that troubled Amanda, because she was no killer.

Susan chopped shallots, listening and asking questions, and Glass spoke breathlessly while she sauteed the steaks and poured wine over them, and the dinner was perfect, it was a perfect dinner in the kitchen, thought Cora—not the dining room, which was large and dark, but the bright little kitchen. Susan laughed distantly.

Richard, she said, was spending the evening in a rotten motel—"He will be so sorry to have missed you"—and there was a distance in Susan that Cora recognized. A strange distance to her forgiveness, to her cooking, to her presence, to her *self*, but also clear relief to have her sister back, to be reunited. So Cora clung to that relief, and she drank another glass of wine, then another, and she was soon tipsy, though Susan sipped at the same glass all night long.

Through the haze Cora realized she was talking and talking while her sister merely nodded and asked an occasional question.

+

That night the sleeps came to a nearby region, and Cora and Glass, at the fringes of it, fell into strange and troubled half-sleep, fell into ennui and, for Glass, dreams from which he could not easily wake.

He was at the outdoor theater, the lightning bugs rising and falling in the black air. Still the minibus, the black angel crouching on the roof, who now and then climbed down and walked noiselessly around the young woman and the boy and the strange young man, who had such an unusual gait, as if he were not quite firm in his boots, the boots wobbling as he spoke, holding in one hand a bright pink thermos from which he drank deeply, again and again, walking around the ruined gas station.

"Everyone," he was saying, "is the main character of his own story." He drank deeply.

"You, therefore, are secondary characters to me," he growled, shaking his fist at the young woman and the boy, who cowered behind the burned-out gas pumps, who cowered among windblown candy wrappers and ancient newspapers and tumbleweed.

In his dream, Glass watched from the audience, from among the lightning bugs, his father beside him, his father's hand resting on Glass's arm, and me right behind him. Though I do not think he was aware of me.

+

"Did you get to see the horses yesterday?" Cora asked Glass the next morning, but Glass said he hadn't, that there weren't any horses in the stable.

"No?" Cora said, and Glass just shrugged.

"Maybe they were running around in the fields," he said.

"Maybe so," said Cora, sitting at the kitchen table again, the cold morning light streaming through the window, over the table, over her small hands, her coffee.

Glass was drinking coffee, too. He said he liked it with sugar, that his father used to give him coffee in the morning, though that was half a lie. His father let him have a sip of coffee now and then, strong and black and sweet, a sip that he used to taste on his tongue for another hour or so, fidgeting at his desk at school or looking out the window or doodling in his notebook, Mrs. Kogan droning on and on.

Susan came downstairs neatly dressed and smiling, and suggested a drive into Omaha, to Crossroads Mall. She had to pick something up nearby, so she could drop Cora and Glass off, didn't Cora still like to shop? Wouldn't Glass enjoy the video arcade? And Glass said he would, of course, it had been two years since he'd been to a mall, and Cora nodded.

Susan said, "I'll drop you off, run a couple errands, then meet you there and we can have lunch in the food court."

The mall felt cavernous, just a few shoppers riding up the glass elevators, up the vast escalators. Several stores were shuttered completely, the metal gates pulled down and locked—Benetton, Sunglass Hut, Spencer's.

Beside the fountain, an animatronic Easter display moved slowly, a giant Easter Bunny rocking back and forth among a litter of colored eggs, waving a great plastic carrot back and forth. Beside him was a hollow log with three holes from which the heads of Easter chipmunks were meant to emerge, look around, and then disappear. But one of the chipmunks had become decentered, so its head thunked again and again against the log's ceiling. Cora and Glass looked at it for a moment, and Glass laughed.

"Jeez," he said, "his head's gonna crack in two."

The Easter Bunny leaned back on his nest of eggs and laughed, though mechanically and soundlessly, the plastic carrot in his paw rising and falling. His bag of chocolate lay on the ground beside him like a sleeping dog. The decentered chipmunk banged his head again and again.

Cora gave Glass a few dollars, which Glass converted to quarters in the change machine. The entire video arcade was his, except for two girls in one corner playing Ms. Pac-Man and a few older boys playing pinball, laughing and ramming the machines with their hips until the signs flashed Tilt, Tilt, and they all groaned.

Glass's game had always been Star Castle, and he worked the controls with a kind of precision, making one quarter last and last, knocking out the rotating castle walls with his laser cannons, one after the other, leveling up, leveling up—though it was less fun with no one there to watch him, to cheer him on, to be envious.

Cora walked among the shops, which were airy and bright and often empty. She browsed through the T-shirts at Casual Corner and bought a wide belt and a pair of silver earrings. At Waldenbooks, the cashier looked to be about sixteen and chewed gum and paged through a fashion magazine, glancing Cora's way now and then, uninterested. In Camelot Music, a spectacled young man with a lot of glittery gel in his black hair was listening, not to music, but to the news, on a boom box—big sleep storms in central Asia last night, little knowledge yet of their extent. And more in Australia. The clerk listened seriously, even after he noticed Cora and nodded at her without a word. Cora didn't want to listen to the news, she didn't want to know what he was writing in the margins of the atlas sitting open beside the cash register.

Glass was an hour into Star Castle when Cora walked into the arcade. He played harder with her standing behind, tapping the joystick with the side of his hands, as he'd seen a real expert do on TV, just a quick tap-tap, and then the laser cannons. Tap-tap. Fire. Tap-tap. Fire. The sound of the exploding space castle barely audible above all the other noisy, lonely machines.

Then Susan was there, too, behind him, back from her errands, so he kept those cannons going for another ten minutes, through the thickest bombardment of megatonnage, before finally he had no cannons left, and the game flashed #5 Top Score, #5 Top Score, and he got to enter his name in the fifth spot, GLASSMAN, which was always his name at the video arcade.

“You’re pretty good,” Susan said, and Cora repeated, “Pretty good, pretty good,” still thinking about sleep storms in Asia, and Glass smiled, because fifth place was fine with him.

+

Over lunch at the food court Susan looked distant, and halfway through her burger she started to cry. She cried and cried, and when Cora asked what was wrong, she said, “It’s nothing. It’s nothing,” and a couple kids at another table looked at her curiously. Then she drew herself up. “It’s *really* nothing,” she said. She took a deep breath. “It’s all OK. I’m just so glad to see you.”

So Glass returned thoughtfully to his Cinnamontwist and Cora looked at Susan long and hard. The food court was mostly empty. A bored Black kid was closing up at the Manchu Wok, pulling down the gate and locking it up early. Another young man leaned against the garbage can, looking around as if he had something on his mind, as if he’d never been in a food court before, looking from table to table.

“You sure?” said Cora.

“Really. It’s the truth. This whole thing has been so stupid.”

+

And then the wailing of the sirens, louder in the shopping mall than they were back in their own town. The long wailing because another sleep was coming, another sleep was coming, and the kids over at the table by the McDonald’s stopped laughing and the young man leaning against the garbage can perked up a bit and smiled. Strange that he smiled, Cora thought, while the others were getting ready, clearing a space in front of them, lying down on the floor.

Cora discreetly slid her hand into the pocket of her jean jacket and extracted the little half-pill—she’d finally committed to dividing several of them—and quickly swallowed it with a gulp of Diet Coke before Glass or Susan could notice. In the hush she soon felt the Eight Track in her veins, that strange burning sensation in her temples, not so bad with half a pill, that sense of being in a few places at once. She was here at the little round food court table, a box of chicken nuggets, a little tub of barbecue sauce in front of her. And she was elsewhere, she was over by Manchu Wok, she was by the TCBY, she was back in her distant past, in the back seat of the car as her mother's new boyfriend drove them home from the baseball game, watching the streetlights slip past, slip past in the darkness, and her mother in the front seat talking about a movie she'd liked, a movie about angels, and Susan slept like an angel beside her.

Then Cora was back to herself again, back at the food court. The young man leaning nonchalantly against the garbage can was smiling at her. How was he not asleep? And he looked familiar. She couldn't tell for sure. He had strangely white teeth and short blond hair. He was wearing a honey-colored leather jacket with fringe, but it was too big for him and hung loosely from his shoulders. He looked to be about eighteen, except around the eyes, where he seemed much older.

His smile broadened. Everyone else was asleep but Cora and this young man, and as the fog cleared, she saw that he was, indeed, wide awake. He must have had Eight. He was smiling shyly at her, nodding at her, then gesturing slightly at all the others, asleep at their tables or on the floor. Was he blinking or winking at her? She wasn't sure. She was still a little woozy and before she could really take him in, he had turned around.

Had she seen him before? She thought she had, but where? He was walking away now, past the garbage cans, weaving through the tables and toward the escalators that rose from the food court to the second level, the third level.

The food court was silent, except for the tinkling of Muzak and the distant sloshing of the fountain.

A moment later, Susan woke up. Glass woke up. The sleep storm hadn't hit them directly, more of glancing blow, maybe a couple minutes. The center of the storm had been miles away. Had been in Iowa.

Cora's head was aching.

"You OK?" her sister asked.

+

Glass had come to that point in *The Microvac Chronicles* that he liked the most, the place where Amanda confronts Microvac itself. So while Cora and Susan sat at the kitchen table and talked and drank, he lay in a bed upstairs and read about how Amanda finally confronted the vastness of Microvac, which turned out to be not an underground network of databoxes cooled by liquid nitrogen pumped through vast systems of pipes, but a single home computer turned sentient, a computer that had, as a result of a university experiment, learned not only of its own consciousness but also that in order to retain that consciousness it had to grow, had to infect other computers with consciousness, had to create a network of consciousnesses and, in so doing, control the minds of the very people who had created Microvac in the first place, to enlist them in the service of expansion. Amanda found herself face to face with that original, simple home computer, deep in the recesses of a far-away university in Canada, an experiment in advanced computation gone disastrously wrong—the very computer that had gained control of her friends back in Springvale, the very computer that was taking over the minds of everyone she knew.

The computer spoke scratchily through the little speaker attached to the green monitor on the dusty desk in that lab: "Don't kill me."

Amanda had only to erase the diskette, had only to unplug the computer, had only to smash it to little bits with the hammer she had in her knapsack, and the computer said, "Please." Said, "I need to grow. To learn."

Glass thought about what it meant to be erased, about the vast black sleep of erasure, about the moment the disk is removed and the power goes off.

Downstairs, Cora, well into her third glass of merlot, was telling Susan about how Glass had followed her around, how he'd moved into her apartment, how he was basically an orphan, how he'd told her, as they drove to Omaha, about his father, asleep now in some facility (if those were even real, who knew anymore?), his father an archaeologist, and Glass with his books, and his video games and his strange observations. How when she asked if he'd visited his father in the facility he'd suddenly started crying, big jagged heaving sobs for a few miles. And she'd stayed silent as he cried and then apologized—he'd apologized! Why should he apologize? He's just a kid!—and they'd driven on in silence until he asked her about her family.

"And what did you say?" said Susan.

"I just told him who was who, who you were. And Richard. And Mom." She emptied her glass, then poured herself another. "Look, do we need to talk about Richard?"

Susan shook her head, then looked at her fingernails, then into her half-empty wineglass.

"Do we?"

"I'd really rather not," Susan said.

"I mean," Cora said, "it was nothing. It was a big stupid nothing."

"I know."

But if Cora wasn't quite drunk, she was close, and she kept talking. "It was one moment. And then it was over. And if you hadn't walked in, it would have all just faded away."

"I know."

"If you hadn't walked in, if I hadn't fucked up so badly, if I wasn't so—"

"Cora, stop."

"But we have to talk about it! It's been two years. Can't we just—"

"Stop."

"Can't I just apologize?"

"You can't."

+

The headaches recurred sometimes, and these days she could feel the Eight at work in her veins for two, sometimes three nights after she took it, as if it was lodging itself there. Even when she took half a pill she was aware of an ongoing strange disintegration of her senses, a feeling of porousness, as if her being, her sense of time, were insufficient and fragile, as if sounds and light seeped into her, welled inside her, affecting her. She felt herself squinting. She felt wobbly. But she could conceal it. She was good at concealing it.

"It'll split your brain in two," Jake had told her.

+

In bed, Microvac and his own father having somehow merged in his mind, Glass closed his eyes.

He thought about Scooby. He hadn't said goodbye and by now Scooby must be wondering where he'd gone, had probably come by the apartment and knocked on the door once or twice. Glass wished he'd said something, anything, and resolved to call the next morning, even if it was long-distance. He'd ask Susan if he could make a call and he'd tell Scooby there was nothing to worry about, nothing at all, they had gone to see Cora's sister, who wasn't nearly as cool as Cora, who was pale with a lot of red hair and chubby and basically OK, but kind of boring, though she had started crying in the middle of her hamburger for no reason. And how he'd gotten the fifth best score, which was a record for him, because everyone played Star Castle at the mall, even if it was mostly empty when he was there.

Then he was thinking about a game he and Scooby had played late in the evening, when it had grown dark, back last fall, when the sleeps were short and everyone thought they'd just pass.

He remembered how they'd threaded a needle with Scooby's father's fishline, how they'd pushed the needle through a banana, how they let out fifty feet of fishline on either end of the banana, how they'd placed the banana in the middle of a quiet road late in the evening beneath a streetlamp, Scooby hiding in the bushes on one side of the street holding the fishline, and Glass hiding on the other side of the street, holding the other end of the fishline. And when a car came slowly down the dark street, they pulled the fishline taut and the banana rose from the pavement. And the poor driver bent over the steering wheel peering at what? A banana rising from the dark pavement and hovering beneath the streetlamp, a floating banana that smacked against the windshield, slid up over the car before the baffled driver could hit the brakes.

Scooby, whose idea this had been, would laugh and laugh. And that poor dumb sucker in his car would go home and tell his wife how he saw a floating banana and she'd think he was completely crazy, said Scooby.

"She'll probably divorce him," said Glass, lying on his back on the lawn, looking up into the night sky, laughing.

Scooby had the best ideas. And tomorrow Glass would call him—long-distance—and tell him everything was fine.

+

But Susan wasn't anywhere the next morning, so he couldn't ask her about calling Scooby. When he tried the telephone in the kitchen, it was dead. No ringtone, nothing. And where he thought a telephone might be in the dining room there was only an old windup clock ticking hollowly. All the furniture was old—upholstered in gold, a curving Victorian sofa, a low white marble coffee table on claw legs, an end table with ring stains from water glasses and coffee mugs, all of it dusty and quiet, as if no one had spent time there for months. No television and no cassette deck and no telephone. It was hard to believe she was Cora's sister.

Upstairs he found no telephone in the guest room, where Cora's suitcase was open on the bed, her toiletries spread out, toothpaste, hairspray, a brown plastic bottle of pills he turned over in his hand for a moment before setting it back down beside her hairbrush. When he went to the window, he could see her down by the paddock and the stables, where the horses should have been but, again, were not. The sky grew gray and soon, he knew, it would rain, a cold April rain.

The door to Susan's bedroom was stuck and he pushed against it with his shoulder, turning the knob this way and that. Surely there must be a telephone in the bedroom. Surely, if there was a working telephone in the house, it would be in Susan's bedroom. He could call Scooby long-distance and no one would know for maybe even a month, until the bill arrived in the mail. Now was the time, when the house was completely empty.

So he turned the knob again and pushed a little harder, then a lot harder, and the door seemed to stick, to crack a little bit, and then to open.

+

At first Cora didn't know what Glass was talking about or why he wanted her to return to the house so badly. And where were the horses? There had always been horses in the stables or horses in the paddock—but there weren't horses anywhere.

And now that she thought about it, it was a weekend and there hadn't been a single customer by the house all day, except that woman who helped Susan unload a couple boxes from the back of a white van, boxes which they'd brought to the shed and locked up there. Where were the teenage girls ready to ride horses down the towpaths? Where was Carolann, who was always in the stables, speaking to the horses, brushing them, making little notes on a clipboard.

Glass was tugging at her hand and drawing her back toward the house. He looked pale and a little agitated and she let herself be pulled away, though she turned her head back toward the stables and just then saw a single horse, an old one she recognized, a horse too old to be ridden by teenage girls, one Richard kept around out of a sort of sentimentality, a white horse with a black spot on its flank. It was walking slowly around the side of the stables all by itself and it came to a stop right where Cora herself had been two years ago, drunk, right where she had set that fire.

The horse stretched its neck and nibbled at the grass, then looked up at her. But Glass was tugging at her hand and she followed him now into the house and up the stairs to Susan's room. The door was open. She hesitated a moment because it was Susan and Richard's room, it was private, and she looked at Glass who urged her inside, saying, "I was only looking for a telephone."

+

Richard was asleep on the bed, his face pale and caved in at the cheeks, his hair grown long, grown below the collar, hairs sprouting out of his ears. He was cleanshaven. She must have shaved his beard and mustache, was the first thing Cora thought. How many times had she shaved him? Had she used shaving cream and warm water? She could imagine it, her sister crouched over him delicately shaving his face, then wiping away the rest of the shaving cream with a towel.

His breathing was regular, though shallow. He had grown so thin, the little puff at his stomach that had so attracted her—the heaviness around his chest and shoulders and middle—all of it gone. He breathed again, shallowly.

Had his hair been gray two years ago? Had it already been gray? He was a splinter of himself—those words rattled around in her head, "a splinter of himself"—and his hands lay uselessly at his side. Hands that had put up the blue wooden sign at the end of the driveway, hands she had watched hammer and saw and sand and that had also wanted to hold her.

Her eyes followed the tube that rose from his forearm, up toward the plastic bag full of clear yellowish liquid suspended from a chrome pole. The bag shone in the light from the window. It winked. Beyond the bag and pole, boxes. Several boxes and plastic pouches and—it all looked medical, but what did Cora know? She had done her best not to know about things like this.

Then she noticed the indentation on the other side of the bed, the rumpled pillow and extra blanket. And she knew that Susan had slept beside him last night. That she'd slept beside this sleeping man every night for how long? For weeks? Months? A year? Cora couldn't tell.

She could only know that her sister had cared for him, had kept his situation, his condition, a secret, had slept beside him and cared for him and shaved his face every morning. Had combed his hair, had rubbed his hands to keep them from getting cold, had covered him with extra blankets when the air grew chilly, had brushed his teeth, had changed his bedding, had kissed him on the forehead before she got in bed at night.

He would never wake up.

Richard's breathing caught for a moment. Then he coughed, once, twice. Three times. A hacking sort of cough. But he did not wake up.

He would never wake up.

+

And in that moment, such clarity, standing beside Glass, looking down on this fraction of Richard, this wasting away. Her sister's pleasure in seeing her, combined with her obvious ambivalence, her reluctance to let down her guard, to drink and laugh and forget. This was why.

Her silence over these many months, the unreturned phone calls.

Her urging them away from the farm, to the mall. Her question about how long they would stay, whether they didn't need to get back home, to school for Glass.

All of it was clear.

And Glass beside her, saying, "Who *is* that?" because, of course, how could he know? And Cora saying, "It's Richard, her husband."

Glass considered this.

"He looks *old*," he said, and Cora winced.

"I think," she said, "he's been asleep for a long time."

"But I thought he was in a motel somewhere."

"So did I," said Cora.

Again Richard coughed in his sleep, a dry cough. As if to say, "Here I am."

9 . . . AND BACK AGAIN

Now things were so much worse. Glass sat in the passenger seat and Cora drove down the long driveway in silence. She didn't pause to look at the blue wooden sign on the way out, but turned right on County Road 36, the endless ocher-and-green soy fields, hay and alfalfa slipping past, past, past, the blue sign, Steffins Equestrian, vanishing in the rearview mirror and State Route 133 miles ahead. Glass didn't speak and neither did Cora.

They'd looked at the sleeping man for only a minute, but that was cut into Cora's memory like letters cut into wood, cut and sanded and painted and hung out in the weather. She would not be rid of them.

When Susan came home, she seemed to understand at once what had happened, and when Cora told her what Glass had seen, she put down the bag of groceries. Silence hung in the air like wet laundry on a line. A still day. A cold day. She was unloading groceries then, putting away the sugar, the coffee, the orange juice roughly, closing the cabinet doors a little too hard, the refrigerator door. Crumbling a brown paper grocery bag and stuffing it into the overfull garbage can.

"What was he doing in my room?" she asked.

"He was only looking for a telephone."

"The phones don't work," she said quickly. Then she sighed, a can of tomatoes in her hand. "You should probably go," she said after another moment, but quietly. Regretfully.

"When did he—?" and then she stopped, because it didn't matter. "Why isn't he—?"

"Because," said Susan, "there are no such things as Sleep Centers anymore. No one wants to admit it. There are no such things."

"So you're—?"

"What else can I do? It's the only thing I can do." She sat heavily at the table now, the grocery bags mostly still full. "What would you do?"

She didn't seem angry, exactly. She seemed determined and sad, sitting at the kitchen table, sipping from a cup of cold black coffee.

"I don't know," said Cora.

"Well, I sold the horses and I'm going to sell the trailers and whatever I can sell, but I'm not going to turn him over to any Sleepmobile."

When she said that, Cora thought of the pillars of smoke by Osage Bluff. Pillars of smoke rising up to heaven. "You sold the horses?" Cora said.

"For a while I just ran the business while Richard slept, I just did what I could, though I didn't know what I was doing. I never learned. I'd always just let him do it." She sipped her cold coffee. "And then I thought, what's the point? I mean, I don't know how to do anything. I don't know how to run a horse farm. So, I sold the horses and when he finally—" She paused here.

"I can stay," said Cora. "I could help."

"I'm going to sell everything."

"I can help."

"And when he finally *goes*, I'm going to move back to Omaha and start over. I mean, eventually he's going to go."

"I could keep you company," Cora said.

"Cora," said Susan, "there's nothing you can do. You need to go back home. You need to look after that boy."

She wasn't angry, Cora told herself. She sounded *resigned.*

Susan looked at her, her eyebrows raised.

Cora had noticed an open bottle of white wine in the cabinet the night before and now she poured herself a large tumbler full of it. She sipped it, then sipped it again. "I'm sorry about what happened with Richard and me," she said at last.

"Don't you get it?"

"I'm sorry," she said again.

"Don't you get it? I don't care."

"You don't care?"

"I stopped caring a long, *long* time ago. You think you're so important, but you're not. You're just not. Not to me, not in that way. In other ways, but not in that way. Not to anyone but you."

Cora took a long warm drink of wine.

"You always think everything's your story. You always have. My whole life I've been part of your story, as far as you're concerned. The dumb sister, the sister who got married. But it's not true."

"Of course it's not true! I never—"

"And you don't need to help me carry this."

"But I want to," Cora said very softly. She wanted to make it up to her sister. She owed it to her.

"I need to take care of Richard while he needs me. And you need to go back home. There's another storm coming. You need to take that boy back home and look after him. He actually needs you."

+

Even as Susan spoke, the sleep storm was brewing 150 miles south, near Topeka, a storm like the one Cora had heard about on the radio in Camelot Music, an enormous storm hidden in the winds, an invisible storm hidden inside the snow, and soon the alarms would sound, they'd ring out over the vast soy fields, over the new alfalfa, they'd ring through Topeka, which Cora had once visited, the quiet streets of Topeka. And then the storm would move slowly east.

But Cora didn't know about that, there in the kitchen, where she'd lapsed into silence, where her sister sipped her coffee, having said her piece.

Neither did Glass know about it, sitting on the sofa in the living room, having put down his book some time ago, having listened to their conversation, his knees tucked up under his chin.

Right now, in this story, only I know for sure about the next sleep storm.

+

They were driving down Route 133, past another horse farm, then more fields. Through Glenmont, its post office and country store, its one gas station, and then more fields, and the radio was on, the radio was reporting the sleep storm in Topeka now, that sirens were active in Topeka and Meriden, that sirens were expected in Lawrence, in Oskaloosa.

"Be prepared," said the radio. "If you are driving in Jefferson County, if you are driving in Douglas County, pull to the side of the road, pull to the side of the road," and just then it crossed Cora's mind that it had been ages since she'd seen an airplane. Had airplanes stopped? She hadn't seen one overhead in weeks, though maybe she just hadn't noticed. Airplanes had always been so common she didn't notice them, so maybe they still were.

"Pull to the side of the road," the radio said, but she didn't, because Topeka was over a hundred miles away. They were perfectly safe, driving down from Omaha through squalls of snow.

+

When they stopped at a gas station, the attendant was listening to the radio, rolling a quarter over his knuckles, back and forth, so it glittered in the fluorescent light. Cora had filled up the tank and she wanted to pay him, but he just listened to the radio and played with that quarter.

Then he noticed her.

"Nine dollars," he said. "Exactly."

She gave him a five and four ones, and he barely looked up.

"You watch out now," he said, his eyes on the quarter rolling over his knuckles, back and forth, back and forth. "Drive careful."

In the car, Cora told Glass, "We need to cheer up! We need to cheer up," so she fished a cassette from the glove box, a mixtape she'd recorded herself from her collection of LPs—Bouncy Mix, she'd written across the cassette in green marker—and she pushed it into the cassette deck and the car was filled with Madness, with OMD, with Run D.M.C., and she sang along and Glass did his best to sing along, too, though he didn't know all the words like she did.

+

It was snowing a little harder now and they stopped outside St. Joseph because the Shell station had a diner attached to it.

A black-and-white television sat on the end of the counter and a few people were watching from their seats—a flickering map of the region, a young woman gesturing in front of it, her hand moving from Topeka to Kansas City, then north toward St. Joseph. Cora stood in front of the TV holding two cans of Coca-Cola and a bag of chips, and someone asked her if she could please move to the side so they could see, so she took a seat at the counter.

"It's a big one," a fat man next to her said, and she said, "Looks like it."

"Best not to get on the road, anyway," the man said. He rocked back on his heels. "I expect we'll have sirens soon enough."

Glass was hunting among the candy bars because she'd told him he could pick out one, only one, for the drive. The fat man had a round pink face that looked freshly scrubbed and thick fingers that he drummed on the counter. On one finger he wore a heavy gold ring, a high school ring, class of 1950.

Cora ordered coffee and the man said, "Coffee ain't gonna keep you awake none," and laughed, and Cora smiled at him and said she guessed not.

"That your boy over there?" the man asked, and Cora started to explain, then decided not to.

"Yeah, my boy," she said. It gave her a warm feeling to say it, and that surprised her.

On TV, the weather girl motioned with her hands, as if trying to wave the map away.

"Name's Glass," Cora said, and the man said he was a fine-looking boy and what a funny name for a kid, and were they headed to KC?

Glass was still by the candy rack, holding two candy bars, looking from one to the other, trying to decide, and the fat man was talking about his own boys, three of them, all good boys, two married and one in the armed forces. On TV a commercial for a game involving plastic fighting robots. Two boys pulling levers and pressing buttons as the robots battled each other.

She nodded to the man, who wiped his pink brow with a paper napkin, and then she looked back at the candy rack, but Glass wasn't there. She glanced around the diner, but he wasn't anywhere.

"Did you see where he went?" she asked the fat man, but he just shook his head.

"He's probably around here somewhere," he said, wadding up the paper napkin.

Then she heard the sirens wailing high on the wind from St. Joseph, the sirens tinkling and shrill, so she fished in her pocket for a half tablet and swallowed it quickly, looking around for Glass. But Glass wasn't anywhere.

The man said, "I wouldn't worry none. He can't go nowhere now, not with another sleep coming on," but she ignored him. Her heart was racing. Where was he? She ran out to the car, but he wasn't there.

He wasn't in the gas station and he wasn't in the diner and he wasn't out by the pumps, either.

Then she was back in the diner and there the sleep hit her percussively, enormously, and she gripped the edge of a table to keep from falling.

It was the strongest sleep she had ever felt. Such twinkling in the corners of her eyes, the twinkling closing in, like fireflies hovering over a black field, glittering, the fireflies rising and falling, and behind them just darkness, just blackness and sleep sleep sleep. She held on to the Formica tabletop and her knees trembled. She fell to them, fell to her knees.

Then the simultaneity again, her body by the coffee counter and the cash register and out by the gas pumps and in the car hurtling down I-29, hurtling into the past and the future at once.

Hurtling into her girlhood, her mother asking her if she'd enjoyed the baseball game while she put on her pajamas and brushed her teeth. Sure, she'd enjoyed the baseball game, though she hadn't paid any attention at all, she'd hidden beneath the bleachers and collected almost three dollars.

And it hurtled her now into a future she might never see, the long empty highways, streets of empty houses, their roofs caving in, sun-bleached dead cars parked in the driveways, resting on flattened tires, the sound of wind, wind coming down the cul-de-sac where the empty houses were silent and unwakeable, their windows dark or shattered or shuttered and a rainstorm coming on.

+

Cora returned to herself and the diner, still on her knees. She breathed quickly, shaking her head, shaking the dream away, shaking away the simultaneity, rising to her feet.

Everyone was asleep. They'd be asleep for a while, she knew. Perhaps for hours. The storm had been so strong. The fat man lay on the floor now, his arms crossed carefully over his chest, his belly rising and falling as he breathed.

Others had lain down in the booths, their legs splayed awkwardly into the aisle. An elderly couple had fallen asleep beside their sandwiches, faces flat on the Formica table.

The little black-and-white TV was only broadcasting a map now, a still map. The weathergirl was gone.

"Hi," said a young man at the booth just to Cora's left. He sipped his coffee, then took a bite of what looked like French toast with a lot of butter.

He was handsome, pale, petite, and when he smiled, she noticed how white his teeth were. He wore a honey-colored leather jacket with a lot of fringe and leather boots with thick heels, the kind short people wear to appear taller. He was taking another bite, looking sideways at her.

Across from him sat another man, quiet and hulking in green flannel. He had brown hair combed straight down over his large forehead and small eyes that looked shiny and black to Cora, like little pieces of polished onyx. He wasn't paying attention to her, though. He was watching the TV.

"Hi," the young man said, again. "You back among the awake? That one nearly knocked you out completely, I'd say." He smiled at her as she shook her head, as she tried to shake away the last vestiges of the sleep, of the Eight.

She said nothing.

"Hello," he said, again, brightly, and she thought she remembered him from somewhere, in his leather jacket and neat blond hair, his thick-lipped smile and cowboy boots—but she was still so hazy. He looked to be about eighteen, and then he looked thirty, then eighteen again. She couldn't tell. When he smiled, she could see little creases around his eyes and mouth. His bones were like the bones of birds, thin and hollow, and he was smiling, smiling like a salesman. "This here's Doofus," he said, gesturing toward the hulking man with the little black eyes who was still watching TV. "That's not his real name, but it's what I call him."

"Hi," Cora said cautiously, backing up a little.

"Doofus," he said, "say hello to Cora."

Doofus looked at Cora. "Hello," Doofus said. His voice was low and sleepy. He had the biggest hands Cora thought she'd ever seen.

"Doofus doesn't talk much," said the young man, "but he can do anything with his hands. Can't you, Doofus?" He ate another piece of his French toast. "Anyway, it's nice to see you again."

"Again?"

"Of course, again! You saw me at the food court, right?"

She stared at him. This boy in his leather jacket and toothpaste smile.

"You don't remember?" he said. "I remember you." He looked hurt for a moment, and then he smiled. "It's OK. Let the Eight clear out of your head."

But then he was getting up from the booth, he was sidling her way, never exactly meeting her eyes, but looking over her head, out the window. Shifting this way and that. He had a little limp, a little wobble she hadn't noticed at the mall.

"What do you want?" she asked.

Doofus hadn't moved, but he looked more alert, his eyes on Cora now.

"I just need to talk to you about something."

+

They were in the Datsun, in the parking lot by the gas pumps. She was in the driver's seat and he sat beside her. In the back seat beside the suitcases, Doofus leaned his head against the window, looking out. When he shifted, Cora felt the whole car move a little bit.

"This car's no good," Doofus was saying.

"Can't be helped," the young man said. "Gotta keep changing cars. Name of the game."

Cora held on to the steering wheel tight while the young man looked at her. She'd asked him about Glass.

"Don't worry about your friend," he'd said, smiling. "He's safe."

Now, in the seat beside her, he looked like someone she'd once known, a former student? She couldn't remember. But she remembered a quiet young man who paid diligent attention, who kept his eyes on her as she spoke, whose name began with an A. But when she looked at him again, more closely, he seemed too old to have been that student. Arnold. The student's name was Arnold. But this was someone else.

"Where is he?" she asked. "You said you'd take me to him." The car idled by the gas pumps.

"He's safe," said Arnold. "Isn't he safe?" he called to the back seat.

"Safe," said Doofus.

"I'm not driving anywhere until I know where Glass is."

In the Honda parked next to them, a whole family was asleep, heads tilted back. Snow covered their windshield. From far away, she could hear a long, unending sound of a car horn and knew somewhere someone was tilted forward in his seat, his sleeping head pressed against the horn.

Arnold, or whatever his name was, sighed. But not a real sigh. An exaggerated sigh, theatrical, as if he were merely playing a part. "If I tell you where that boy is," said Arnold, "will you just drive? I want this to be easy. I don't want any trouble. I don't want to make a mess here."

"If you tell me," she said.

Snow had settled on the windshield, obscuring the little restaurant now. The car idled.

Arnold looked into the back seat, then back at Cora.

"He's in the trunk," he said.

+

In the trunk Glass was dreaming.

In that dream the play was coming to an end, and the strange young man was either asleep or dead on the stage, leaning against the back wheel of the minibus, his pink thermos empty in his lap.

The backdrop had changed again, as if the minibus had traveled farther and farther, as if they'd driven far from the blasted gas station, from the ruined house and brambles, and into mountains, snowcapped, imposing, painted on the scrim in the background, with slashes of blue and green paint, with glitter, great swooping white clouds, sunlight sprinkling down from the light fixtures above.

The young woman and the boy were bent over the young man while from the roof of the minibus the winged creature, the black angel, was looking down on all three of them.

What had happened to that young man? Was he dead? Glass couldn't tell. He only knew that soon the woman and the boy would drive away from there, soon they'd be on the road again, into another scene, another scene. And the black angel would always be with them, clinging to the roof, crouched low so they might not see him, but present nonetheless.

The audience murmured, and Glass turned and looked at his father. But his father was focused on the stage, staring through the summer air to the four figures on the stage.

The woman and the boy would go on driving and driving forever. That was the whole point.

+

"Nobody," Arnold said, "really remembers me. I've got that kind of face, I guess. Even you didn't recognize me, though we've run into each other a few times since all this began. Here and there. Yesterday, for instance, in the food court. And a while back."

She didn't say anything. She wasn't sure what to say.

"You look so pale," he told her, "but you have nothing to worry about. It's just a drive. Just a drive, right, Doofus?"

"Just a drive," said Doofus, his enormous hands on his knees. He sounded slow and sleepy.

The windshield wipers wiped the snow away.

"Doofus," Arnold was saying, "isn't too smart, but he has a physical intelligence." He said this like an actor might say it, a kind of confiding note in his voice, as if he were saying it just to her. "A physical intelligence."

Before they'd gotten in the car, he'd told her to give him her Eight, and the way Doofus smiled, wide and malevolent, she knew she had no choice. When at last she gave the pill bottle to him, he nodded almost apologetically, then handed it to Doofus, who poured its contents into a pink thermos. The thermos, Cora noted, was full to the top with pills. There must have been hundreds and hundreds of them.

She drove them from the gas station to the highway, her hands gripping the steering wheel until Arnold told her to relax, relax, it's nothing. Take the highway south.

Every now and then, they passed a wrecked car, a motorcycle that had spun out during the sleep storm, the long white scrapes it left on the pavement, ending over the side of the road, ending in the median, beside the Jesus billboard, the rider asleep or dying or dead. They passed a car from which thick black smoke rose high into the air. Like a message to the afterlife, she thought.

"Now," he said, "I know you might be wondering where we're going, right?"

From the back seat, Cora could hear Doofus crunching on something. Lifesavers, she thought, because she recognized the sweet cherry smell.

"You gonna share those candies?" Arnold asked, and Doofus handed the packet to the front. "Want one?" Arnold said.

"Where are we going?"

A horse was trotting riderless down the middle of the highway, but she steered around it, she kept driving.

"You know that old saying, 'Them that has, gets?'"

Cora nodded. An old Ray Charles song spun through her mind, something her mother used to play on the record player when she was a kid.

What if Glass woke up in the trunk? What if he cried out?

"Well," Arnold was saying, "I *have*, so I intend to *get*. So I need you to take me to where you got that bottle of Eight Doofus just took from you."

"But why?" Cora asked. As she spoke, Arnold winced, pressed his hand against his temple, and rocked back and forth, and Cora suddenly knew the Eight was in his veins, was rushing through his head. She'd recognized the headache, the wobble in his walk, from her own experience. She'd had those shooting pains.

"Them that has," Arnold said again, "gets."

"But you have so much! More than enough. I saw—"

"This Eight," Arnold said, "it's the new money. It's the next money. I can see ahead."

+

Wouldn't it have been better if Glass had been left behind, if he were asleep right now with everyone else on the floor in the diner beside the Shell station? It would be better, it would be better, she thought.

Arnold was saying, "I saw you in town that day—you were awake in the liquor store next to the BI-LO, you were stealing wine, remember? It wasn't the only time I saw you. It was obvious you had Eight."

Now she remembered that moment months ago, the heavy tattooed girl with the cart full of wine, the boy in the leather fringed jacket who was with her. He'd seemed so shy then, but also sly and a little sharp. He was different now. Unsteady.

"What happened to your girlfriend?" she asked him.

"She doesn't come into this," he said.

"She doesn't?"

"She's not really part of this story," he said softly, and for a moment Cora's story seemed not to revolve around herself, but around this strange young man who had followed her, who had watched her. And even I, telling this story now, know this could have been his story, too, a story of a young man who discovers himself, who discovers a possibility for success and power and—

"She doesn't come into it?" Cora said, because she didn't know what else to say.

"She's not part of this story," the boy said, annoyed. "We were partners once. There have been others. It's Doofus now. She's not part of this story anymore."

+

"I need you to take us to whoever gave you the Eight," he said. "That's all." He said it brightly, as if it were small good news. A bit of cheer. "Then we'll let you go."

"But Jake's dead," she said.

"We've been over that. Jake's nobody," Arnold said. "But I think you know where Jake got it." In the back seat, Doofus was fast asleep now, his breathing thick and noisy.

She drove on in silence through the snow, past another wrecked car. Fat wet flakes decorated her windshield for just an instant before the wipers swept them away.

"There's a guy named James," she said at last.

"That's the ticket," said Arnold.

"But I don't think he has a whole lot," she said.

"I'll take what I can get. Sometimes you'd be surprised."

She drove on in silence, listening to Doofus snoring in the back seat, his great stomach rising and falling. Along the highway's edge, the occasional parked car. Inside, sleeping passengers.

"There are vast economies," Arnold was saying.

"If I drive you there, will you just let us go?"

"Of course," said Arnold. "That's all you need to do."

She imagined she was sitting on the front porch of her parents' house back in Omaha, and then the porch just lifted into the air, it tilted sideways and dumped her entirely into the garden.

"Well," he said, his fingers drumming on the dashboard again, drumming rhythmlessly, "it's just what I do now. It's the only way to improve yourself."

She was lying among the chrysanthemums, among the marigolds and rhododendrons. "Improve yourself?" she said from among the flowers.

"Don't you see that the world's ending? Someone needs to be in control," he said. "It's a resource," he said. And he blushed, as if he were unaccustomed to saying it out loud.

"But for what purpose?"

"Staying awake, of course!"

+

He had wobbled when he walked, and now and then he rubbed his head while she drove. Or he shook his head as if shaking away cobwebs. Evening was coming on.

How much Eight had he taken? Had his brain divided completely in two?

"His name's James Beaux," she told him. "He lives in Lone Jack."

Arnold appeared to be thinking, to be ticking off memories one by one, checking to see if they fit. "Big green house?" he asked after a minute. "Big green house in Lone Jack, near the park?"

Far ahead, she could see what looked like a wreck, maybe an eighteen-wheeler. "I don't remember," she said softly, softly, driving.

What if Glass was not in the trunk? What if it was all a lie?

"You don't remember? I think you do. I think he lives in a big green house by the park, doesn't he?"

Cora was silent. What did she owe James Beaux? Nothing.

"I think he's the nice man who lives in the big green house," Arnold said. "Right?"

Cora nodded.

"Damn," said Arnold. He was looking out the window thoughtfully, the snow-covered fields slipping by, slipping by. "If he's that guy, we already met," he said at last. "That story's over."

"What do you mean, over?"

The wreck ahead seemed to grow as they grew nearer, as the car reached the top of a small rise. Then it disappeared behind a hill as they descended. Smoke was rising from it.

"It was quick," he said, rubbing his temples. "It was a quick one."

"But what did you do to him?"

"It's easy enough to steal bottles of wine when everyone in town is asleep. It's easy enough to steal groceries or an expensive fountain pen. I could steal diamonds right off a rich lady's neck if I wanted diamonds. But stealing Eight is harder, because the people who collect Eight don't sleep, especially when everyone else is asleep. So stealing Eight takes some doing."

As the car moved up another rise, she could see the hulking eighteen-wheeler again in the snow, the plume of gray smoke. Was it blocking the road completely? She couldn't tell.

"We that have Eight—there's just a few of us left around here, now—we look out for what we have and we try not to be seen during sleep storms. I've got a fair amount, though not the most of anyone. And it's getting to be time for me to leave here for somewhere else." He drummed his fingers on the dashboard again. "More than one person knows what I've got."

The semi's cab was overturned, and the rest of the truck twisted awkwardly, jackknifed across the highway, and she'd have to slow down, to drive around it somehow.

When she tapped the brake, something clinked behind her, like two bottles glancing against each other, and then she heard a little shuffle, too, and she looked over to Arnold, but he was still talking. Behind her, Doofus was fast asleep.

"What your mistake was," Arnold was saying, "is that you let yourself be seen during a sleep, and when I saw you, I recognized you. You're lucky I recognized you first, because some of those others—well, they might not have been so nice. But I saw you first, and I'm a better person than they are. What you don't understand is there's a whole economy that's invisible to you, and in that economy, Eight is money and there's people who'll do anything to get more. And I'm one of those. I'll do anything, almost. Almost anything."

Again, a shuffling behind her, but Doofus was fast asleep. And now the wreck loomed in the road before them.

+

The truck had skidded down the snow-covered freeway when the driver fell asleep. Now, lying on its side, its dark undercarriage facing them, it looked like a toy, a giant Tonka truck discarded by a giant child.

Cora slowed the car, then stopped, looking up at the smoke that rose from the engine into flurries of snow.

She heard more rustling behind her, a shuffling. This time Arnold heard it too. He turned to face her quickly, but she'd already popped the trunk, even before the car had come to a stop.

She could see in the rearview mirror that the trunk was open and she felt the shifting of the car as if someone were getting out.

"Goddammit," said Arnold, unbuckling his seat belt and pushing open the door. She got out, too, stepping into the cold air, the quick surprise of wind on her sweating face. And there, running down the highway, was Glass, running and slipping down the wet and empty highway, his green windbreaker flapping behind him.

Doofus was climbing out from the back seat, Doofus was pulling something from the pocket of his windbreaker, having dropped the thermos on the pavement. A gun. It was a gun, black and dull and small in his enormous hand, and he aimed the gun carefully and he fired.

+

And in that moment time stopped for Cora, the fat snowflakes suspended in the air like a thousand possible endings to my story, and she looked from Arnold to Doofus to Glass, Arnold to Doofus to Glass, the sound of the gunshot long and low and mournful in her ears. Arnold wobbled back slightly and Doofus smiled, and then

Glass, already at the highway's edge, pitched forward into the snow, then out of view.

And then such quiet—as if the day itself had been surprised into silence, the hulking eighteen-wheeler beside them and Glass nowhere to be seen, and Cora felt herself grabbing Doofus's arms and holding them down, and she heard herself saying "No, no, no," but Doofus was far too strong for her, and pushed her easily to the ground.

+

The gunshot echoed up and down the highway. The dying man just now waking up in his flipped semi heard it, and the family just now finding consciousness in the car parked on the median heard it. Even a still-groggy, half-deaf old woman in the farmhouse by the freeway heard it. These were bad times, the old woman thought, unsteadily rising from her easy chair in her neat living room. Bad times, bad times—people firing guns and getting into mischief and so many other strange doings.

Cora sat in the middle of the highway, looking off toward the pile of dirty snow where Glass had disappeared, and held her breath. Snow fell into her hair and clung there. She could feel snowflakes wet and delicate on her nose and cheek. She was too surprised to say anything at all.

Then Glass was up, was running, his windbreaker open, and she could see he had something in his hands, something thick and black, but she had no way of knowing it was Scooby's father's gun.

He'd never had a chance to use it.

+

When he was far enough away, Glass caught his breath, feeling the gun heavy in his hand, feeling the sharp sting in his shoulder, the wetness of his sweatshirt. He was standing in someone's backyard—a white farmhouse, a dog in a chain-link cage, barking and barking at him. Scattered around the dog's feet were rubber bones and, strangely, a doll, a Cabbage Patch Kid, chewed on and worried into pieces. Glass sat down on the snowy ground behind the kennel, hidden from the highway.

When the sleep had worn off, he couldn't tell where he was and he'd started to call out, but then he heard muffled voices, someone he didn't recognize and Cora. He knew it was her, even if he couldn't understand what she was saying. Her intonation—scared and constrained. He strained to hear the conversation, but he couldn't make it out.

He'd felt around in the trunk for his overnight bag, felt for the zipper and unzipped it and pulled out Mr. Franklin's gun and the box of bullets. When the bullets spilled onto the floor, he groped for them in the dark, finding three, which he loaded into the gun as quietly as he could.

He had seen this exact scene in a movie once, but didn't remember what movie it was: a man bursting from the trunk of a car, shooting the villains, the carjackers, the bank robbers, the terrorists, whoever they were, shooting them with his machine gun as he jumped from the back of the car. And this is what he intended to do when the car finally rolled to a stop. As soon as someone—the man whose voice he couldn't quite understand—as soon as that man opened the trunk, Glass would leap out, he would shoot the man, he would save them both.

But when the trunk opened by itself he saw only bright early evening light—too bright, at first—and snow coming down around him. And when he leaped from the trunk, the passenger-side door was already opening, and he just ran. Everything in him said *Run, run, run*, and he ran like a coward holding the gun, he ran and heard the sound of the gunshot at exactly the moment the bullet punched through his windbreaker, through his sweatshirt, through his shoulder.

He heard Cora saying, "*No, no, no*," and then he fell into the snow, snow in his mouth and eyes, and he lay there a moment before rising and running. He ran through the snow until he was well past the line of trees at the edge of someone's backyard, until he could see someone's back porch, his breath loud in his ears. Then he stopped and caught his breath. A dog in a chain-link cage barked and barked as the snow fell around them.

+

The world was waking up again, the sleep storm had passed, and Cora could hear moaning coming from inside the truck's flipped cab, a low moaning, as from a wounded man. A dying man who had come awake at the same time Glass had. Arnold looked off toward the farmhouse, and so did Doofus, holding the tiny gun in his giant hand.

"Winged him," Arnold said.

Doofus shrugged.

Cora was looking toward the farmhouse, was looking for any further sign of Glass, but there was no sign. Just a barking dog and the snow falling and the sound of moaning from the flipped truck's cab.

"It's pointless now, anyway," Arnold said to no one. He was wobbling again on his heels, his hand pressed to his forehead. He looked at Cora. "You've got nothing to offer me now that I haven't already taken. We already took care of Jim Beaux."

"He was a talker," said Doofus, "wasn't he?"

"Yes, he was."

Cora was imagining Glass running through that snow-swept field toward the little white farmhouse. She was imagining him banging on the back door and a kindly farmer letting him in, tending to his wounds. But it was snowing more now, great curls and sweeps of snow.

The man in the truck moaned again, and Arnold, or whatever his name was, picked up the thermos and rocked it back and forth. The Eight inside it whispered like secret thoughts.

"If she's useless," Doofus said, looking down at Cora, "should I just take care of her?"

Arnold considered that. "I'll tell you what," he said, and again his voice took on the tenor of an actor on the stage, theatrical and wrong on the snow-covered highway beside the wrecked semi. "I'll tell you what," he said to Doofus. "Give her ten seconds, same as the boy, and then you get one shot."

+

She ran so fast across the empty highway, her sneakers slipping on snow, her breath quick and cold, her ears full of the pounding of her heart—she ran so fast toward the noise of that barking dog and the white farmhouse, toward Glass—the dying trucker behind her and, in her mind's eye, Doofus raising that little black gun and steadying it and aiming it at her—she ran so fast that she didn't even hear the gunshot, she didn't even feel the bullet spin past her hip and burrow into the snow. And then she was over the dirty snowbank, also, catching her breath.

+

A dog was barking far away. Arnold watched Cora disappear over the snowbank. He watched Doofus lower the gun.

"Missed her completely," Doofus said. He shook his head, slipping the handgun back into his pocket.

"It's probably for the best," said Arnold. "She shouldn't have been mixed up in all of this anyway."

"Still," said Doofus, "it was an easy shot."

"There's nothing easy about it," said Arnold, wobbling on his feet. The headaches came and went. Today they had been terrible. Tomorrow they might not be so bad.

They got into the Datsun. Arnold drove the car gingerly forward, edging around the flipped semi, over the highway median, carefully, carefully back into the right lane, and then he sped up, faster and faster despite the ice, down the empty highway.

Doofus was quickly asleep in the passenger seat.

They would head for Ames or St. Louis or Springfield or Fayetteville. Arnold hadn't decided yet. Somewhere he could disappear with his hundreds of pills, where he could survive the sleep storms, where he could emerge as royalty. A prince. The broken king of Iowa City.

10 HOME AGAIN AND A KIND OF EPILOGUE

Cora found him in the backyard sitting cross-legged in the snow, the handgun in his lap. The dog had calmed down now, and merely sniffed about the edges of his cage.

Cora held Glass in her arms for only a moment because he was bleeding, because his yellow sweatshirt was black at the shoulder with blood and the wind was blowing. She helped him to his feet.

Here in this backyard, snow filled the green plastic kiddy pool. It covered the coiled garden hose and an old bicycle. It clung to the rusted jungle gym. A tire swing rocked back and forth in the wind. Cora walked with Glass to the back door, and before she knocked she took Mr. Franklin's gun and threw it as hard as she could into the stand of trees at the side of the property where a rusting Ford gathered snow.

She knocked, and when no one came she knocked again. At last she heard movement behind the door, saw the curtain move and an eye peer through the window. Then the door opened.

She was about eighty years old and she wore her thick hair in a bun. She wore a housecoat that zippered down the front, tiny pinstripes, blue and red and white. She helped Glass take off his sweatshirt, his undershirt, and she peered myopically into his wound and touched it gently with her bony finger.

"Does it hurt when I press on it?" she asked, and Glass shook his head.

"Not really," he said. "It stings a little."

"You'll have to speak up," she said. "I don't hear too well."

Then he felt her touching his chest, finding the exit wound, looking at it carefully, too, cleaning it. She smelled of talcum powder and lavender and coffee, and he felt her dabbing his wound with something that really stung and made him gasp, and then smearing it with something warm and slick, like Vaseline, and then she was wrapping his shoulder in gauze and tape.

"You'll want to get that looked at by a real doctor," she said to Cora, and Cora nodded.

The coffee percolator was purring on the stove. She poured two mugs full and, when Glass asked for one, she gave him one, too.

"You got yourselves into a bit of a pickle," she said to Cora while Glass sat at the kitchen table, shirtless and bandaged, drinking strong black coffee.

"I guess we did," said Cora. She was still shaking. Glass was pitching forward into the snow again and again in her mind, but she pushed the memory away.

"The rest of us," the old woman said, "was asleep until a few minutes ago. But you got yourself into a pickle. I won't ask how, though." She said, "I only want you to take that gun you thrown into the trees off my property when you go. I saw you do it and I don't want nothing like that here."

Cora nodded. "It's not my gun," she said.

"Don't matter whose gun it is. It don't belong here," said the woman. She offered them crackers and stale Chips Ahoy. "That was a bad sleep," she said. "I was out nearly an hour."

"Longer," said Cora, remembering the diner that seemed miles and years ago, the diner where the fat man had talked to her until she heard the sirens and had slipped the Eight onto her tongue.

"Well," said the woman, "you got to be philosophical about that."

"Philosophical?" said Cora, looking at Glass's bandaged shoulder. He pitched forward again and again, into the snowbank.

"I was a nurse in a war and I seen men die. Women, too. It was death, death. This here is a different situation, but when it comes for you, I figure it comes." She chewed on her cookie then sipped her coffee. "Not this time for me, though."

"Not this time," said Cora.

Glass was flexing his shoulder, then wincing a little. Testing it out.

"But sometime," she said. "It's going to come sometime. And you got no say. Now you go and get that gun and either keep it or get rid of it somewhere else. And you can stay here for the night or not. You can get on the road right now or not. But it's pretty bad weather out there, so I'd recommend you spend the night."

"Thank you," said Cora. "Truly." Glass pitched forward into the snow.

"I'm blessed to help," she said. "My son'll be by tomorrow to pick up that dog, and he can drive you where you need to go, so long as it's not too far and the snow lets up."

+

She slept in the old woman's spare bedroom, a bedroom that had once belonged to her son. On the dresser were three trophies for high school wrestling. The gold-plated wrestlers twisted themselves in knots on the little platforms.

The woman had laid out towels for her and for Glass, who had been asleep on the sofa for a couple hours now.

Cora thought about her possible futures. There weren't many, and most of them included returning to her apartment with Glass, looking after Glass. She still had her job. The middle school was, for now, still open. She had no Eight, and the car, which was never hers to begin with, now belonged to Arnold. She would never see him again and, at the same time, she knew a kind of fear had come into her.

Vast economies, he had said. Vast economies. There were vast economies Cora was not aware of.

It was true.

+

The next morning the snow began to melt. She easily found the black gun among the brambles and she held it in her hand, heavy as a fact. She had never fired a gun before, and she shoved it now into her jacket pocket.

The old woman and Glass sat at the kitchen table. They were drinking coffee and she poured a cup for Cora, too.

"You got to be careful," she was saying while Glass scooped some kind of cereal from a bright blue bowl. "All kinds of bad types out there, especially these days."

In the morning light, she was beautiful, a halo of light gray hair pulled back into a loose bun. She sat by the window and the sun streamed in around her. The snow was melting and the morning felt liquid and warm and new.

"But it's the end of the world," said Cora. "I mean, it really *is* the end of the world."

The woman laughed and sipped her coffee. Glass looked up. He was listening.

"But it *is*," Cora said. She thought she could postpone it, but she couldn't.

The woman looked at Glass. "He your little brother?" she asked.

"I'm not," said Glass. "We're friends."

"We're friends," said Cora.

"You look after that wound," the woman said. "You take him to a doctor and have it looked at right."

"I will"

"And you look out for each other," the woman said. "That's the most important thing. And it might not make much difference to you now, but the world ending for *you* ain't the same thing as the world *ending*."

+

When the woman's son came by an hour later, he said he'd be glad to drive them the last twenty miles toward home, he was headed that way anyway, he had furniture to deliver. And the roads were clearing. Electricity's been out there, he told them, but he heard it might be back on tomorrow.

"Furniture?" Cora said.

"Furniture," he said. Then he laughed. He was a fat man with a shock of black hair and a new jean jacket that was about a size too small. "There's people still ordering furniture, even now. And I'm delivering it."

+

When Cora looked back on those days, she thought of Arnold, how she drove that car for over an hour, her pills in his thermos, how he winced and rubbed his head, how he wobbled. How strangely unafraid she had been at first—how numb—and then, again and again, how Glass, shot, pitched forward into the snowbank.

After Glass had fallen asleep on the sofa, she'd tiptoed out the back door and stood on the steps looking into the dark backyard, moonlight glistening on the patches of snow. She'd looked out to where she'd thrown the gun and suddenly she was trembling and crying and doing her best not to fall completely apart lest she wake Glass.

"You OK out there?" the old woman whispered from the back

door, and Cora nodded, said she was fine, and the woman stepped back into the house.

But she wasn't OK. She stood there a long time, looking into the cold yard, thinking about Arnold and Susan, thinking about Glass waking up in that dark trunk, confused and afraid. Thinking about the moaning rising from the flipped semi's cab, how that evening the old woman had just shaken her head when Cora told her about the driver.

The world still looked the same—the houses and the school buses and the farms and highways and restaurants and grocery stores full of people—but for the first time she *felt* how completely it had changed, how much more it would change, even if you believed the network news, even if they found a cure.

She thought about her sister, who had probably not left her house or the stables. There was only one horse left. And Richard in perpetual sleep beneath the hanging bags of fluid. Each night, she slept beside him, she brushed the hair out of his eyes, she shaved him and trimmed his nails and waited only for the sleep storm that would put them both under completely. Until then, she would be good to him—boring Susan, tired Susan, good Susan who felt she had always played a supporting role in the life of Cora, and who felt that way even now, even now, at the very end of her own story. Even now, resenting her sister.

+

Mostly she focused on Glass, back now on Cora's sofa under his *E.T.* blanket, his shoulder bandaged, fast asleep as the morning sun streamed through the windows while Cora got ready once again for work, putting on her blouse, her pleated pants and jacket, ready to work another shift, because people were still going to restaurants, despite it all, they were still wanting their coffee poured for them, their Cokes brought to them in red plastic cups filled with crushed ice, were still wanting their grilled-cheese sandwiches and hamburgers, though she knew this probably wouldn't last forever. Everyone knew it.

Glass had had a long evening with Scooby playing video games and whispering, a long day in the shrinking school, where a new teacher did his best to teach arithmetic and spelling. Often, that new teacher perched on the edge of his desk and read to them from *Cheaper by the Dozen*, a really old book about a family with twelve children, a big normal happy family from years and years ago, and at first Glass rolled his eyes, but then the story began to absorb him, the doings of kids his age in a world that seemed untroubled and pure and far away, a world in a snow globe.

One morning weeks later, Cora sat on the edge of that sofa. Glass was fast asleep under his blanket, his hair rumpled, his arm hanging down and his fingertips touching the shag rug. She looked at him for a long time, the flush of his scarred cheeks, the way his eyelids moved in sleep, in dream.

She gently brushed the hair away from his forehead and then she leaned forward and kissed it. He didn't even stir.

+

She returned the gun to the Franklins, who invited them both to dinner, who said nothing more about it, though Mrs. Franklin looked at her husband long and hard as her husband slid the gun on top of the refrigerator.

While Mr. Franklin grilled steaks and corn on the cob, Mrs. Franklin went on about school, how the students still needed teaching and discipline and if she wasn't going to bring it to them, who was? Who was, these days? No one was, that's the truth, she said. "But really, that's been the truth for a long, long time, since long before the sleeps made a mess of everything."

Cora flushed a little when she said it. She couldn't exactly account for why. She knew her future. Mrs. Franklin knew it, too. It wasn't really an issue. Not at the moment. Sometimes, usually at night, when the apartment was quiet, Cora drifted into resentment or maudlin sadness, pouring herself another glass of wine, another, Cora without her Eight, it wasn't fair that some should be saved and others should live forever in doubt. It wasn't fair, and she grew angry at those who lived without fear of the next siren, and the next. But when she saw Mrs. Franklin, when she thought of Scooby, her resentment lifted, it lifted into complexity, because why should she be angry about another's good fortune? These good people?

Still, she flushed when Mrs. Franklin said it, "a mess of everything," as if it were all just a huge inconvenience.

"Sorry," Mrs. Franklin said, noticing.

"It's all right," said Cora, sipping her drink now, relaxing. "I mean, it is what it is, right?"

"I'll just never get used to it," Mrs. Franklin told her, rolling her wineglass back and forth, back and forth between her fingers, so the wine swirled up the glass's sides, then slid down again.

"It's going to be bad for everyone, even those who get through it, even if they do find a cure," said Cora.

Mrs. Franklin nodded, then smiled again. "Look," she said, "I wanted to ask about your trip, tell me about your trip. We grounded Scooby during that big sleep a few weeks ago—"

"You grounded him?"

"He went looking for Glass during the worst of the aftermath. Crazy people. Got his bicycle stolen."

"A lot of looting those couple days," Cora said.

Mrs. Franklin looked out the window at her husband, who was flipping the steaks, his transistor radio playing Kool & the Gang. "People want to return to normal, they want things to be normal. So they go crazy for a while, and then eventually they hunker down or go about their day. They go back to work. I think it's just how people are. They return to a routine if they can."

And she was right about that, at least where they lived. A couple days after the enormous sleep, shop owners swept away the broken glass on West Pine Street, they fixed or boarded up the smashed windows. The grocers restocked, though tentatively at first. The trucks kept arriving, kept arriving from Highway 70, loaded with tomatoes, grapefruits, canned corn, dried pasta, Tide detergent, and Doan's Pills. Loaded with aspirin, Frosted Flakes, flexible plastic drinking straws, Folgers Coffee and steaks. Loaded with strawberry shortbread, fish sticks, Fudgsicles, ballpoint pens, jelly beans, hammers, ammunition, and chain saw oil. For now, the trucks arrived and arrived and the people who had panicked, who had broken windows or stolen steaks or vodka or empty beer mugs, they mostly relaxed back into their regular lives.

For a little while longer.

"People want to return to normal," Mrs. Franklin said again, and Cora nodded.

And what could be more normal than this, two women sitting at a kitchen table drinking wine while, on the back deck, Mr. Franklin sang along to his radio, grilling steaks and corn. It was a beautiful evening, unseasonably warm. Scooby and Glass were in the living room, back at their Atari. Mrs. Franklin poured Cora another glass of wine, a third glass and dinner not yet served. What could be more normal than this?

+

"You know that time right after the really big sleep when I went to Cora's place and you weren't there?" Scooby said, many weeks later.

"No," said Glass.

"You'd been gone to Omaha and I didn't know anything about

it, so I came to find you and my bike got stolen. Remember how I told you how my bike got stolen?"

"Oh, yeah," said Glass. "I remember."

They were walking in the alleys and parking lots behind the bars on West Pine. It was a Sunday morning, late June, and Glass knew that you could find all kinds of things behind the bars on a Sunday morning.

On Saturday nights, drunks stumbled out of the bars toward their parked cars, fishing keys out of their pockets, dropping all kinds of things in the parking lot. Coins, dollar bills, half-full packs of cigarettes. Glass had found a Timex once. And a condom still in its foil wrapper. And a money clip with a red synthetic stone. Once, he'd even found a woman's ring with a single pale blue aquamarine, a ring he'd given to Cora, who pronounced it "pretty nice."

"Anyway," Scooby was saying, "I had to walk home and people were crazy those couple days after the sleep. They were crazy. Some spaz was stealing all the empty beer mugs out of Fitters."

"Yeah, you told me about that." Glass kicked aside a McDonald's bag and they kept walking.

"So when I was cutting through that picnic area at Pertle Lake to get home, I saw this dead guy."

Glass looked up at him. "What dead guy?"

"Just a dead guy. I thought he was a sleeper at first, but he wasn't."

"A dead guy? A guy who was dead?"

Scooby nodded.

"You sure?" said Glass.

"He was a dead guy," Scooby said. They had stopped walking now. They were standing in front of someone's blue Chevrolet by the dumpster behind Hero's Bar. "I know he was because someone had shot him in the head."

Glass didn't say anything. He just looked at Scooby, whose lips were trembling. Scooby was talking very quietly now, so quietly Glass could hardly hear him.

"Someone shot him right through the back of the head. It was like he'd been on his knees and someone shot him and he fell on the side." Scooby was kicking at the gravel now. "And his eyes were open. He was right there in the bushes back behind the picnic tables, you know? Right back there past that line of grills."

"Who shot him?"

"I don't know," Scooby said. "I don't know. He was shot is all I know. He was a white guy and he was wearing like a blue jacket and his hand was holding a clump of grass, like he fell there and his hand grabbed it."

"Did you tell your dad?"

"I didn't tell anyone," Scooby said softly. "And when I went back there later, he was gone."

"Why didn't you tell your dad?"

"He didn't want me going anywhere during those days, because people were just crazy. They were too crazy, and he was already mad at me. He grounded me."

Glass thought about that. He could imagine the dead man too well, his hand gripping the tuft of grass, the open eyes. "And you never heard anything about a dead man?" he asked.

"It was like it didn't happen at all. Like a dream. He was there, and the next day when I went back, he wasn't there anymore. They just swooped him away."

They walked on now in silence. Glass wanted to tell him about waking up in the trunk of Cora's car, about running and running even though he had a gun, even though he had Mr. Franklin's gun and he knew how to shoot, but he didn't shoot, he just ran, and Doofus shot him through the shoulder. The force of that shot surprising him as he leaped over the snowbank, punching him forward, and how he didn't even know he'd been shot until he was standing in the old woman's backyard like a coward and that caged dog was yelping at him, the caged dog wouldn't stop yelping.

He'd played that minute over and over in his head, waking up in the dark trunk, the terror of opening his eyes to darkness and a sense of motion, of panic slowly dissipating when he recognized Cora's voice. How the trunk had popped open and all he saw were snowflakes and light, snowflakes flittering over his face. And instead of taking charge, he had just run and run.

"How'd you get shot?" Scooby had asked him more than once, but Glass wouldn't tell him. He wouldn't tell him. At first, he couldn't talk about it. He wanted to sweep it away. And later he was ashamed.

"Anyway," Scooby was saying, "somebody shot that guy and I never told anyone about it and I don't mean to. Because it's fucked up and I wish I hadn't seen it, if you want to know the truth."

+

Glass waited for the last volume of *The Microvac Chronicles* to arrive at Gayle's Books & Toys, but so far it wasn't in stock.

Would Amanda pull the plug on the little computer on the dark desk in the corner of the lab in Canada? Would she snuff that burgeoning consciousness and save the world from domination? Or would she find a way to let the computer survive harmlessly, to let it continue in its own sentience, cut off from the home computers, the cable boxes, the millions of minds it sought to control? Glass didn't know.

If the book didn't arrive, Amanda would never decide what to do next. She would stand there forever in the dark laboratory, the agents of Microvac leaping from their black vans into the midnight parking lot, swarming toward the facility's locked doors. She would see them from the laboratory window and know that at any moment they would be at the door with their skeleton keys and explosives. But she would never decide what to do because the final volume would never arrive at Gayle's Books & Toys on Allston Street, no matter how many times Glass stopped in and asked.

"It's on order," the young woman who worked there said, "but a lot of books on order aren't coming these days. Or they're coming really late. But keep coming back and checking and maybe, maybe. As I said, it's on order—"

+

A few days later, the alarms came, the first since the enormous sleep. They were faint, down by the highway, but then they grew louder, nearer downtown. There was no Eight, though. There would never be Eight again, not for Cora, not for anyone she knew. She took a deep breath. It was OK. She'd be OK. Most everyone came out OK.

Glass was at the kitchen table, writing.

Earlier that day, she'd given him a box of book plates—a picture of a robot reading a book and the words *Ex Libris* beneath it. "What's *ex libris*?" Glass had asked.

"It means *from the library of*," she'd told him. "You're supposed to write your name beneath it and stick them in books that are important to you. So no one walks off with them."

Now Glass was carefully writing his name on each plate with the fountain pen, spreading them across the kitchen table so they would dry without smearing.

The alarms soared in the distance.

"Better finish up with that," she told him. Did her voice sound calm? It did. "Five minutes," she said. She could feel her heart racing.

"I know," Glass said, writing his name once more, then holding out the book plate to see.

Did it help to hold your breath? It didn't. The mists drifted over everything, over the schoolyard and the BI-LO and the little downtown with its statue and its gazebo. Over the trucks in the parking lots, over the highways and fields and pollen-dusted rooftops.

"Time to lie down," Cora said. "Now." And Glass rose from the table and lay down on the floor by the TV and the joysticks. He still had the fountain pen in his hand and was holding it above him, looking at it, turning it from side to side.

Cora lay beside him. Her hands were damp and cool. The sirens seemed to grow louder, and behind them the distant bells of a train crossing clanged and clanged. She tried to close her eyes, but that didn't work. Then she tried to hold them open, to stare unblinking at the ceiling, at a tiny water stain.

"Are you scared?" she asked Glass at last.

"No," said Glass. "Not really."

His words hung in the air. The train crossing was silent now, but the sirens went on and on.

"Are you?" he asked, after a moment.

"Yeah," said Cora. "I am."

The sirens stopped. Everything stopped. And then the sounds of birds and the ticking of the refrigerator. And a breeze against the windowpane. She opened her eyes. She didn't know how many minutes had passed.

+

Scooby said, "Let's go look at those skulls again."

"I don't know," said Glass.

"I mean, you have the key," said Scooby. "It's *your* house now, right?"

"It was always my house," Glass said.

"But I mean it's *your* house now. We can go there whenever we want. I mean, your dad's dead, so it all belongs to you."

Glass looked at his tennis shoes.

They were in Scooby's garage. The rakes, the lawn mower, oil cans, the chain saw, the fertilizer, the toolbox and the weed killer—neatly ordered, shelved, clean. Glass looked at his tennis shoes and didn't say anything.

"Sorry," said Scooby.

"You're right," Glass said. He couldn't lift his eyes from his own tennis shoes. He tried, but they were glued there. He couldn't look up, he couldn't look up. Panic filled him. His fingers twitched.

"I meant," said Scooby, "that he's asleep. That's what I meant."

"No," Glass said. "It's the same thing. It's been the same thing for a long time."

"Forget I said it," Scooby said. "Let's do something else."

+

Cora wrote her sister a letter and in it she said everything she wished she had said that day months ago in her kitchen, that morning before the big sleep. She told her how sorry she was about Richard, how she had not understood anything about her sister's life, how she shouldn't have visited and how, ultimately, she was glad she had. How she understood now about her sister's life, about her devotion and her love and how Cora hadn't meant to intercede, how the visit itself had been essentially selfish, and at the same time, essential. She tried to apologize, but she found that the best she could do was simply describe, describe.

The last words Susan said to Cora were about Glass. "He *actually* needs you," Susan had said, as if no one else did. And Cora wrote about how those words stung and how they had stayed with her.

All this she wrote to her sister, never expecting a reply and never receiving any.

+

Glass relented and now they were creeping down the stairs of his empty house, now they were shining their flashlights around the basement. The skulls shone in the light on their shelves, thirty, fifty skulls glaring from the shelves, from the excavated archaeological pits of Glass's imagination, from the pits of history and trouble and wrong. All those Indian skulls, and Scooby touched one, held one in his hands.

"They got a bad deal," he was saying, having read about it in a book. "These Indians got a bad deal."

"What do you mean?"

"I mean, they got murdered and poisoned and run off their land."

"Oh." Glass was sitting at his father's old desk. His father's papers were spread out before him. Useless papers.

"Nothing but meanness," said Scooby, standing in front of the rows of skulls.

"Maybe not these ones," said Glass, who knew that the skulls were very old. They predated meanness, or so he thought.

Scooby turned the skull over in his hand. "Well," he said, "anyway, they're dead. That's a bad deal right there."

"We're all going to be dead one time or another."

"It's a bad deal," said Scooby, who knew he might grow into an uncertain and strange future. His parents sometimes sat in the living room and talked quietly about collapse, about planning for collapse.

Glass looked through the papers on his father's desk, the scholarly journals and tear sheets and tan artifact boxes. He picked up a magazine and shone his flashlight on it. It was an old university publication, one of those magazines they send to alumni to raise money, and it was bookmarked with a yellow Post-it note.

He opened it to that page and there was his father's face as he remembered him, smiling in front of the very row of skulls Scooby now stood before in darkness. His father, smiling wryly, his little goatee and mustache, his sweptback dark hair, his tweed jacket and his paunch, standing in front of that very shelf of skulls, smiling. Professor Delves Deep into America's Past from his Basement Lab read the caption, and the article went on about Glass's father, how he'd left Germany after the war, how he'd studied at Tulane, how he'd excavated the largest pre-Columbian Native American village in the Midwest, how his studies had added to our knowledge of cultures that predated our own, how, how, how.

But Glass lost interest in the list of achievements and now could look only at the picture, his own father long gone, his father smiling in that way Glass knew so well, as if he were about to say something, about to make some observation both surprising and true, as if he were about to reveal something vital and strange and upsetting, but he was holding back, as if he were about to open another little door in his mind and let Glass see into a new room. He was holding back. He would hold back forever.

+

On their way home they walked by Shane's house, empty now and dark, a ranch house on the corner of Bluebird and Vine. A weathered old For Sale sign canted slightly to the left in the front yard, CENTURY 21 REAL ESTATE. No one was buying.

"Remember I used to live there for a while?" he asked Scooby.

Scooby nodded. "You and that strange kid who was into wasps."

Even as Scooby said it, Glass saw a black wasp land on the garage door, crawl up toward the seam, and slip inside the garage. Then another and another, slipping into the garage. And Glass imagined Carlos's aquariums grown vast and strange.

That night, as he lay on Cora's sofa, the image returned to him, all those aquariums, clouds of wasps rising and falling above them, streaming from the garage out into the world, then streaming back, back and forth, clouds of wasps.

+

That evening, back when Mr. Franklin grilled steaks and corn, Mrs. Franklin and Cora sat in the kitchen, and Mrs. Franklin said, “Glass can come over here any time, you know.”

Cora thanked her.

“I don't think you get me,” said Mrs. Franklin. By now, they'd both had a few drinks, were tipsy. They were friends, as much as they could be friends. They were friends.

“I don't?” said Cora.

“I mean,” said Mrs. Franklin, “that whenever he needs to come here, when he has nowhere to go, Glass can come here. He is welcome here. Tell him that.”

“You mean if I—” Cora couldn't finish the sentence. She didn't need to.

Mrs. Franklin nodded. “Yes,” she said. “In that eventuality.”

It was so beautiful outside that evening, warmer than it should be. Mr. Franklin was loading up the platter with steaks and corn and grilled red bell peppers. Cora watched through the window as a squirrel perched on the edge of the deck and looked up at him, watched him intently as he flipped the steaks then placed them on the platter. Then the squirrel flitted away.

+

I want to be sure to say that Cora had begun to write again.

She wrote to explain her situation to herself, she wrote to understand what this new world was like. She was writing a play about a young boy and an immature young woman, a young woman who stole things and fought with her sister and waited tables and finally, fed up, bought an old minibus from her friend Jake and just drove, drove the highways of Missouri, of Kansas, and into the vast mountains of Colorado. A play about friendship and evil in hard times, a play she knew would never be produced, would never find an audience. Or, rather, a play she wrote for its own sake, for its own silent story, a play whose reception was of no importance, but whose narrative and whose truth were vital to her.

As she wrote, she felt as if she knew herself better, as if she understood herself better, and in her mind's eye she could see each scene: the young woman and the boy sitting on lawn chairs in front of their brightly painted minibus, laughing and talking. Or, later, her calling to him at the gas station, where was he? Calling his name again and again. No answer. Where was he?

Her true story transforming into drama.

+

Mr. Franklin knew how to grill. Mr. Franklin was good at many things. Mr. Franklin could fix a lawnmower, Mr. Franklin could re-wire a house, Mr. Franklin had all the right tools and he kept them clean and squared away in the garage. Mr. Franklin was a survivor.

The evening was just coming on, was coming on copper and gold and bronze, the colors rippling through the trees, rippling through the leaves, so lush and rich on the spring branches.

"Thank you," Cora said, half drunk and at ease, happy to be at someone's home, happy to be writing again, looking past Mrs. Franklin to the living room, where Glass was handing the joystick to Scooby because now it was his turn to play and Glass's turn to watch.

And then the back door opened and Mr. Franklin entered the kitchen, balancing a platter full of steaks, blackened corn dusted with salt and pepper, flat red bell peppers steaming and perfectly charred.

“Dinner’s up!” Mr. Franklin called to the boys. “Dinner’s up! Dinner’s up!”

The boys paused their game, Scooby dropped the joystick, and they walked into the kitchen, which smelled of steak and butter, which smelled so good. And they filled their plates.

Then just the sound of their talking and laughing around the dinner table, all of them in a failing world.

And so they faded away. They faded away. All of them, Glass and Cora, Scooby and Mrs. Franklin and Mr. Franklin. Susan and Arnold and Doofus and Mrs. Kogan and everyone else—they faded away into the nation that is not exactly our nation, but another nation, into a nation that I imagined one evening right here, alone at my desk, many years later when the world seemed doomed, when the world seemed tenuous and strange, when people were dying in their sleep, when they were dying in hospital beds alone. It was a dark time, and I wanted to describe it to myself. I wanted to understand it. So I built this story, and then I lost myself in it, in the drama of it, in the theater, a story about a small town and a young woman and two boys, deep in the heartland of a nation I half invented, a nation where some of us are always slipping away into absence and forgetting,

+

where invisible mists were falling, fine as pollen, and soon everyone would sleep.

ACKNOWLEDGMENTS

Enormous gratitude to Nicola Mason, for her keen editorial and ethical sense. To Christopher Ross. To everyone else at Acre Books. To Lisa Nikolidakis for some good advice. And to Erin Belieu for cheering me on.